POUNCED:

The Sierra Files, Book 1

CHRISTY BARRITT

Copyright © 2013 Christy Barritt

All rights reserved.

DEDICATION

This book is dedicated to all of my readers who keep asking for more. Those are the words a novelist loves to hear!

A special thank you to Kathy, Janet, Carolyn, and Shannon for your help with this book.

CHAPTER 1

"I'm Sierra Nakamura, and I'm here in the Great Dismal Swamp in Southeastern Virginia. I'm here to tell you about a problem that everyone should know about." I paused and stared at the camera for dramatic effect. "The disappearance of the Hessel's Hairstreak butterfly."

Chad lowered the camera and gave me a "what the what?" look. "Wait, aren't you overstating a bit? I mean, *everyone* should know about this? It's a butterfly."

I scowled at my boyfriend. Why couldn't he see how important this was? This was a beautiful creature on the brink of extinction. "I'm not overstating it. This is a growing problem of which people need to be made aware."

His head dropped toward his shoulder in exasperation. "It's a butterfly. And good job not using a preposition at the end of your sentence."

I sighed and brought a hand to my hip. "Cut the tape."

"It's all digital. There's no tape." His eyes sparkled. He loved getting under my skin. And he was good at it.

"You know what I mean. Don't make me regret asking you to come out here and help me." Truth was, no one else would trudge through the swamp to help me make this video. I'd begged all of my colleagues at Paws and Fur Balls, but they'd all feigned excuses as to why they couldn't come. They had protests to organize. Riots to start. Undercover investigations to perform. Even my colleagues, apparently, didn't see the merits of butterflies.

To me, butterflies represented all that was good in this world. They stood for the chrysalis of change, the beauty of dreams, the transforming power of hope in our lives.

"Did you just say, 'Don't make *you* regret it?' How about *me* regretting saying yes?" He slapped another fly on his neck. "If I see a bear, I'm out of here."

Sure, bears were wildly popular in this desolate stretch of swampland. It was an ecosystem of its own out here, filled with murky puddles of black water, indigenous plants, drapes of moss covering low hanging branches from cypress trees. Our chances of actually seeing a bear were low.

One thing was clear: We were outsiders here. Nature had staked its claim on this land, and we were invaders on foreign soil.

"I'll take a shark to a bear any day." Chad's voice sounded scruffy, which matched his surfer look. His nose was peeling from too much sun. His "soul patch," as they called it, was getting just a little too long. His hair was bleached from hours of being at the ocean, and he wore an old tank top that looked like it had been around for at least a decade.

I rolled my eyes. "Whatever. And just swat the flies away. You don't have to kill them. There are kinder ways of doing things."

"I'm for real when I say this, but rest assured I'm saying it with the utmost affection." He stepped closer and tucked a lock of my hair behind my ear. "I will never understand you, Sierra Nakamura. Flies are a menace.

You're the only person I know who thinks it's evil to flatten one. Next you'll be trying to save mosquitoes, too."

"Mosquitoes have a purpose in our ecosystem—"

He cut me off with a quick kiss.

"Never mind." Chad shook his head. "This nature that you know and love so much is eating me alive. I guess it's more important that bugs survive than if *I* survive."

If I were honest, I kind of wanted to swat at a few flies myself. Not that I would ever admit it. But between the heavy humidity, the glaring sun, an uncooperative crew (that would be Chad), and bugs that surrounded me like I was road kill, I felt irritated.

Guilt flashed through me for a moment when I realized just how miserable Chad was out here. I was so fortunate to have him in my life. We truly balanced each other out. He was hardly ever serious; I was always serious. He had not a care in the world; I had every care in the world. He laughed at problems; I drew on every ounce of my energy in an effort to fix them. Somewhere in that place called "Polar Oppositeville," we'd fallen in love. I was pretty sure that arguing and snipping at each other was our love language.

I had other things to think about at the moment, though. "Let's get this over with." All this talking just meant the longer we'd be out here. I could have this over by now if he would stop arguing.

"I still don't understand why you're doing this. You're an animal rights activist, not a conservationist. I totally get trying to stop animal cruelty. What I don't understand is trying to stop nature from having its way."

"There's overlap between my job and conservation. Besides, Sage Williams was supposed to do this, but she left us high and dry."

"What do you mean high and dry? You mean,

we're in the swamp sweating like pigs and she's not?"

He thought he was *so* clever. "No, I mean she didn't show up at work on Friday, she missed that event we had on Saturday, and she still didn't come in today, which is why I'm here. She probably found another job that she liked more. Maybe it even paid more. She was so flighty. I knew we couldn't depend on her."

I couldn't stand unreliable people. These butterflies were depending on someone to speak for them. That person was supposed to be Sage, and she'd let them down.

Sage always seemed distracted. She missed work more than she was there. And, unlike the rest of the employees, she didn't bother to try and work collaboratively on projects. No, she liked to do her own thing.

Chad raised the camera. "Ready to take two?"

"Absolutely." I pushed a black hair behind my ear and sucked in a deep breath. I had won a debate match my junior year at Yale. I could do this video. It would be put on the Internet and linked to our website. My hope was that it would go viral.

I launched into my spiel about the importance of these butterflies and how since a hurricane and a fire in the Great Dismal Swamp had wiped out a majority of the Atlantic White Cedars, which were the butterfly's primary habitat, these beautiful creatures were becoming endangered.

I ignored the flies that nosedived at me. I ignored the decaying stench of the swamp surrounding me. I blocked out the blistering, wet heat that made me feel like I was swimming through the air with every movement.

For the final shebang, I decided to lean against a downed tree behind me. It was what all the great documentarians did on TV. They looked smooth, at one with nature, in their element.

Only I aimed wrong when I leaned in. The root was more brittle than I thought, and it crumbled at my touch. That small, simple act led to me falling downward and hitting a patch of murky water.

"Whoa!" Chad put the camera on a nearby stump and grabbed my arm. "This is going to be a smelly ride home. Are you okay?"

"I'm fine—" Just as I started to say the words, I looked down at my hand and nearly screamed. "Leech!"

I grabbed the slimy little sucker, pulled it off of my skin, and threw it as hard as I could into the wild. I frantically searched for more, sufficiently freaked out and absent of the usual cool I prided myself in.

When I looked up, amusement danced in Chad's eyes. "A leech, huh?"

I shuddered again. "Yes, a leech. A blood sucking leech."

He stepped closer, shaking his head with exaggerated concern. "How about the poor leeches? Certainly there was a kinder way to treat that poor creature." Chad flashed a satisfied grin.

"Please don't tell a soul that I just did that. My reputation would be ruined." Seriously—the thought horrified me.

He kissed my forehead. "It makes you seem more human."

"I seem perfectly human now." What wasn't perfectly human about giving your every breathing moment to saving the lives of creatures that couldn't speak for themselves?

"That could be debatable."

I scowled, knowing it was time to change the

subject. "Okay, Smart Alec. My glasses flew off when I fell. Help me find them. Please."

Of course, it was hard to find my glasses *without* my glasses. Thankfully, Chad was with me. I really hoped they hadn't flown into one of those puddles. I got shivers just thinking about sticking my hand into that water. Mostly because of, well . . . leeches!

He squatted down and parted some grass to look for my plastic frames. "This reminds me of a scene from Scooby Doo. You know, when Velma loses her glasses and everyone is searching for them. Only, that's usually when the bad guy comes in and starts chasing them."

"The difference is that there's no mystery here. The reasons these butterflies are disappearing are noted and logical."

He parted some more grass. "Don't you think that nature just sometimes takes its course? I mean, is the world going to be that much worse of a place if there are no butterflies?"

He would never understand, and frankly I was tired of explaining. "Let's just find my glasses and get out of here." I stepped over a puddle of water, grabbing a tree trunk to steady myself. My skin still crawled when I thought about that leech. Blood sucking devil.

Still, I shouldn't have thrown it. I should have responded in a more levelheaded manner. I'd work on that.

"Do you see them?" Chad asked.

I shook my head. "They might have flown over there." I pointed in the distance.

I looked beyond the huge oak tree that had fallen. Its root system was probably twelve feet wide, and the roots stood on end like Medusa's snakes. "If I can just get over there."

"By the way, there's something I want to talk to you about later."

I glanced back at Chad. He was down on one knee. He almost looked like he was proposing. I mentally laughed at myself. He was just searching for my glasses.

What surprised me was that my heart had actually raced there for a moment. I fingered the grass around the ring finger of my left hand. Chad had made me a "ring" out of sand reed during a walk at the beach last night. He'd just been being silly and spontaneous.

Then why was I still wearing it? Why did I smile every time I looked down at it?

I remembered that Chad had said something, and I hadn't responded.

"Sure, we can talk later," I muttered. "What's on your mind?"

I leapt across another patch of black water and reached the other side of the tree. There! My glasses lay lopsided against the tree trunk.

"It's something I've been thinking about for a while now," Chad said.

I grabbed my frames, slid them on my nose, and blinked a few times as my surroundings became clearer.

That's when I screamed.

Sage Williams hadn't found a better job.

Sage Williams was dead.

CHAPTER 2

I sat at my desk, staring at the wall in front of me. I tried to concentrate on the faded white paint, but instead, all I could see was Sage's dead body.

Dead bodies were my friend Gabby's specialty. Not mine. I preferred fighting for the lives and wellbeing of innocent animals. Gabby, on the other hand, had started as a crime scene cleaner and recently gotten a job with the Medical Examiner's Office. Budget cuts had cut her new career short, but I was sure she'd be back to acting as a professional investigator in no time.

I'd been back at the office for an hour. After finding Sage, Chad and I had called the police. They'd come out along with a whole crew of forensic people, an ambulance, and even a fire truck. They'd taken our statement, asked lots of questions, gotten our contact information, and finally let us go home, get cleaned up, and return to our day.

Chad had to get back to work with his crime scene cleaning business. With my best friend and his partner out of town for a vacation—the first I'd ever known Gabby to take—he was especially busy this week. He probably shouldn't have taken time to even help me out today, but he'd been gracious.

In return, I'd promised I'd go to a barbecue with

him and not say a word about all the animals people were eating there, each of the guests not giving a second thought to what those creatures had gone through to go from the farm to their grill. But, oh no, I wouldn't be the one to bring it up. Nor would I show them pictures. Nor would I try to fundraise for my efforts.

For once, I'd try to be normal.

Maybe that's why my friend Gabby and I got along so well. Normal wasn't in our vocabulary, and neither of us cared. That made us a friendship match made in heaven.

"I heard about Sage." My coworker Kyla stopped by my desk and peered at me, obviously hungry for some gossip. The woman was in her early twenties and her long, slick hair matched her body, which was tall, thin, and gangly. She had a hippy vibe going and always had enough time to talk about office scuttlebutt.

"Terrible, huh?" Kind of like that puppy mill I'd discovered a few weeks back. I was still trying to wrap up that investigation.

"Who would do something like that?"

I shrugged. "Your guess is as good as mine. If I had to take a guess, I'd say Sage wandered into the middle of a drug deal. I've heard they happen out there in the swamp. It's the perfect place for it because no one is there except for some bugs and bears. A drug dealer's dream."

Kyla leaned closer. "You heard about that fight that Sage and Donnie had, right?"

I shouldn't be curious. I shouldn't ask. But I did anyway. "What fight?"

"Yeah, it was just last week. I came in early—hard to believe, right?—and I could hear them arguing all the way from the parking lot."

To hear it from the parking lot was unusual. The small office space lent itself to many overheard conversations when you were inside. But outside? Wow.

I lowered my voice. "What were they arguing about?"

"I wish I knew. I just know that Donnie was screaming at Sage, and she was screaming back."

"I don't think I've ever heard Donnie scream at anyone." Donnie was the capuchin monkey of the human world. He was Mr. Mild Mannered and even dressed the part, often wearing neutral colors that made him easy to overlook. He was in his late thirties and, though his forehead lacked hair, his eyebrows and the rest of his body had an overabundance.

Kyla shrugged. "Well, the façade we put on out in public is sometimes at odds with who we really are."

That was an interesting statement for Kyla to make.

Facades weren't my thing. Not to sound full of myself, but you pretty much got what you saw with me. I wouldn't have it any other way. Life was too short to keep my mouth shut or to not fight for what I believed in.

I looked over by the reception area, separated from our desks by a glass door with two glass panes on either side, and nodded toward the man there. "I see that Rupert is paying his biannual visit to the office."

Rupert had started Paws and Fur Balls and officially served as CEO. I didn't know much about him. He was pretty laissez faire with us, more of a numbers guy than a crusader when it came to running the company. He concentrated mainly on fundraising for us.

Whenever he was in the office, we all put on our best work faces. Except for right now. At the moment, I didn't even care if he noticed I was staring absently into space. I had bigger worries—like the fact I couldn't get Sage's dead body out of my mind.

I glanced over at Sage's desk. That's when I saw the picture of her . . . cat.

I stood so quickly that my chair flew out from beneath me and collided with the desk behind me. "Mr. Mouser."

"What are you talking about?"

"The police are probably at Sage's apartment right now. They're most likely going to take Mr. Mouser to the pound, where there's already an overflow of cats needing a home. He'll have no hope of survival. Besides that, the poor thing probably hasn't eaten for days."

Kyla's hand went over her heart. "How could we have forgotten about Mr. Mouser? We work for Paws and Fur Balls. We're all about the animals. What a disgrace."

"You're telling me." I grabbed my purse. "I'm going to go over to her apartment and check on him."

"Godspeed, dear one. Godspeed."

***

"Sierra!"

I paused in the parking lot. Uh oh. This wouldn't look good. I knew exactly whose voice that was, and now I was going to have to explain why I was cutting out early on my job.

I turned and waited for Rupert to catch up with me. He was a short man in his early fifties with thinning brown hair. He was a sharp dresser, could give a killer protest speech, and he was a master schmoozer. His life seemed to be his work and, as far as I knew, he'd never been married or had children.

He was the definition of an entrepreneur and had started more than one business. He oversaw several of them now, but was fairly hands off with Paws and Fur

Balls, probably because we were the organization, as he said, that he'd started with "his heart" and not for the paycheck.

That could be because there really was no paycheck. No, we depended on donations from concerned donors from across the country. That meant that this job was mostly a labor of love, and I was okay with that.

My parents, on the other hand, wished I had a more stable, reliable career where I could build a nice nest egg. They also wished I'd settle down, start a family, and come to visit them up in Connecticut more often.

"I wanted to catch you before you left. How's it going?" he asked.

I pushed my glasses up higher on my nose. "I can't complain. Especially not after seeing Sage." Morbid, but true.

"I heard you found her. I'm sorry to hear about what happened to her. I only hope the police can find the person who did this." He paused. "They don't think this has anything to do with her job here, do they? She hadn't made anyone madder than usual, had she?"

Sage was known for pushing buttons and being diehard and focused—when she actually showed up at work. I was no expert on people—not even close—but I definitely hadn't figured Sage out. She was almost—almost—the kind of person I could see secretly planning some dastardly deed to prove her point, something that would land her in jail and ruin the reputation of the company. There was reason for Rupert's concern.

"She had been working some kind of undercover assignment, but she didn't talk about it a lot. She was afraid people here in the office were too chatty." People like Kyla.

"I hate to hear something like this has happened to

one of my employees. You know I think of you all like family." He shifted. "There's one thing I can't figure out, though. Why didn't she take anyone else with her on the Hessel's Hairstreak assignment?"

As touching as his words sounded, I knew where this was going. Rupert was worried about public relations for the company. I supposed that was his job.

And I supposed that I needed to be diplomatic here. "Probably because no one else wanted to go with her. For several reasons. First of all, everyone is busy with their own projects."

"So, she recorded herself? Don't we have it in the budget to hire someone to do it professionally?"

I shook my head. "Things have been tight. Anyway, she was probably using her phone. I'd guess it was stolen after the crime was committed. Makes sense to me, especially if the video might have given away anything about the bad guy." I said "bad guy" with air quotes, feeling like there should be a better word. However, perp or suspect just seemed too intense or like words that should be reserved for law enforcement officials only.

"I only wish she'd brought someone with her. Maybe none of this would have happened if she had."

Or they could have both ended up dead. I kept the thought silent.

"This isn't actually what I wanted to talk to you about." He put his hands into his pockets and jangled some change there. "It's actually about Paws and Fur Balls. I feel like we need a leadership change here. Between you and me, I think Bryan is getting burned out."

Bryan had been the Executive Director of the company for the past ten years. I wondered if Bryan knew that Rupert thought he was getting burned out. I had to agree with Rupert, though. Bryan hadn't been acting like himself lately. He'd run off our office manager Bernard, as well as three other employees. Maybe the man was going through a midlife crisis or something. He really needed to get a grip on things.

"Okay." I had to approach this cautiously.

"Let me just be straight with you. I want you to take over, Sierra."

I pushed my glasses up on my nose again. "Me? I'm . . . I'm honored that you would consider me."

"I really think you have the passion for the company, Sierra. I can see that animals are your life and that you'd do anything to protect them. That's the kind of dedication I'm looking for."

"I'm flattered." And I wasn't easily flattered.

"I think we're cut from the same cloth. You have great ideas, the dedication to follow through with them, and the common sense to know where to draw the line." His hands came from his pockets. "So, you'll think about it?"

"Of course. I'll think about it."

He offered a tight smile and a handshake. "Great. I'll be in touch then."

***

Thankfully, I'd been to Sage's apartment before. We'd met there to plan one of our rallies. It wasn't too far from the Paws and Fur Balls' headquarters. Speaking of which, if I were to become the new Executive Director, my first order of business would be to change the name. I would change it to something more respectful, something like HIPA—Humans for the Intelligent Provision of Animals. Or maybe The Sierra Agency. There were all kinds of possibilities.

I quickly traversed the roads and pulled up to a boxy building with faded yellow siding and wooden steps traveling upward to second and third story apartments. Sage's home was on the first floor.

The police swarmed the place. I ignored them, acting like I knew what I was doing, and charged toward the front door. I went to knock when an officer stepped forward.

"Can I help you?"

Before I responded, I soaked in the interior of Sage's place. It was a disaster. She wasn't always the neatest person, but I knew this went far beyond her normal messiness. Someone had been here and ransacked the place. Interesting. That seemed to kill my random, Sage-walked-in-on-a-drug-deal theory.

I cleared my throat. "My name is Sierra Nakamura. I'm a friend of Sage's, and I would like to take care of Mr. Mouser until someone else comes forward and offers to have Mr. Mouser as their animal companion."

"Mr. Mouser? Animal companion? You mean pet?" The police officer stared at me.

"Pet is such a derogatory term, don't you think? Animals should be more than that." I pointed to his black leather shoes. "They should be more than a comfortable pair of loafers, as well."

"Whatever, lady." He stared at me like I was two floppy ears short of being a character on *Looney Tunes*. "Who's Mr. Mouser?"

"The cat." Sometimes police officers were so dense. I'd dealt with plenty of them in my day, mostly at protests.

"The cat. Of course. It took us an hour to corral that rodent from the closet shelf where he'd holed himself up. Let me get him for you." He returned a moment later and thrust the cat carrier into my arms. "Here. The captain said he's all yours. But he's got one mean, nasty temper. The feline already scratched my hand." He rubbed a bandage there and scowled.

I wiggled my finger into the cage. "Hello, sweet kitty."

The cat meowed in response and stayed at the back of the carrier, his tail twitching. Mr. Mouser was a tabby with brown and black stripes across his coat. He wore a thick collar with skull bones embroidered on it. Right now, his green eyes stared at me. I took that as a silent "thank you for saving me from the horrid police officer."

"He seems fine to me. He could probably sense your hostility." I pulled the cage back away from the officer. "I'll make sure he's taken care of."

As I was walking toward my car, a conversation between two officers on the lawn drifted toward me. "Get this—there is no Sage Williams."

"What do you mean? She's not in the system?" another officer asked.

"No, I mean, there's no record of her existence period."

"Maybe she's in witness protection." The officer laughed, as if the idea was absurd. "With our luck, the feds will be called in. They can ride in on their white horses and save the day."

I'd heard enough.

I was not getting involved in this. Nope. I just wanted to take care of Mr. Mouser and put the rest of this behind me.

CHAPTER 3

I dropped Mr. Mouser off at my apartment, went back into work for a few hours, and finally decided to call it a day.

As I stepped outside into the parking lot, I realized it was already dark outside. Another day gone, I mused, as my shoes clacked against the asphalt.

I checked my phone as I walked to my car, making sure I hadn't missed any calls. It was past eight, and Chad was supposed to come over after work. I'd already called him and told him I was on my way.

I couldn't wait to see him. It felt so good to date someone who actually got me. Even though he wasn't a vegan—he actually loved eating meat, for that matter—he was always quick to help when I needed him. I could handle the meat thing as long as I had his support.

We'd gotten to know each other when I showed up at a dolphin stranding at the beach and saw he was there. He'd been out surfing and volunteered to help. I had no idea he had any interest in working a crisis like that.

Though we'd met seven months earlier, that dolphin stranding had been the first time we'd socialized outside of our normal little group of friends. Chad had fit right in with the crew on the beach. He'd made them laugh while also taking the situation seriously. When I saw him talking to the dolphin, whispering words of comfort to him, I knew Chad was much different than I'd thought.

When we were done, we'd taken a walk along the beach and grabbed pizza—at a vegan establishment, of course. Chad and I had talked the entire time. We'd laughed. He'd promised to show me how to surf. I promised to show him how to start a successful email campaign sure to draw national attention—not that he had need for that, but he'd listened as if he did.

We'd talked about our families, our upbringing. It turned out that both of our parents had wanted something different for our futures than the careers we were currently in. In our own ways, we both felt like a disappointment to them, but we knew we had to be true to ourselves.

Being together had felt easy. It had felt right. Something in my world and in my heart had changed that day.

That had been more than three months ago, and we'd been inseparable since then. When we weren't working, we were together. And we were happy. He'd helped clean some ducks when a chemical spill happened at a local fertilizer plant. We did a Clean the Bay day together. He was all about the beach and preserving its beauty. I could even overlook that he was more of a dog person than a cat person.

Back in the present, I climbed into my car and cranked the engine.

That's when I heard something behind me. Before I could turn to see what the noise was, I heard a click. Something narrow and hard pressed into my side.

My skin prickled. I knew what was happening. Someone was in the car with me. He had a gun, and its barrel was pointed at my ribcage with a straight shot to my heart.

"You're going to do something for me."

"I am?" My voice trembled. Stupid voice.

He jammed the gun harder.

"I mean, I am! Of course." Sweat lined my brow. Where should I put my hands? In the air? On the steering wheel? I couldn't think clearly. Instead I left them where they were—suspended above my legs.

"You need to find the information," he whispered.

Did I know that voice? I didn't think so. The man was obviously trying to disguise it. His rasp sounded purposefully low and soft. "What information?"

"Don't play dumb."

"I'm not. I'm a very intelligent person. Playing dumb is hard for me—"

He pressed the gun into my skin with enough force that I yelped.

"Shut up. Stop talking. I'm not playing. You're the only one who knew Sage well enough to know where she put the information. I want it back."

Was it my imagination or did he say "Sage" with disdain?

"I didn't really know Sage that well, though." He was sadly mistaken, but I had a feeling I wouldn't be able to convince him of that.

"Tell the police and I'll make you pay."

My throat tightened. "Okay."

"Have the information for me by Friday. Otherwise, I'll be back. I'll have my gun. And, next time, I'll use it for its intended purpose."

"You'll shoot me," I mumbled.

"No, I'll shoot your cats."

With that, he slipped out of the car and disappeared, leaving me with the dilemma of a lifetime.

***

That evening, Chad leaned his head back into my couch and closed his eyes. He looked exhausted. I knew his job was physically demanding, but I guess he'd had a lot of work to do today. He hadn't counted on being questioned by police after we'd found Sage. The whole experience had eaten into his work time.

I hadn't told him about the man in my car yet. I was waiting for the right time.

He'd come over to my place after his last job. I lived in what used to be a grand old house in the Ghent neighborhood of Norfolk, Virginia. Since the house's glory days had ended, the building had been cut up into five little apartments. The area was fun, filled with interesting restaurants and interesting people. I liked to think that this part of town was filled with people who thought outside of the box. That made it a perfect place for me.

Chad had brought a sack of fast food with him. I made myself a chickpea salad wrap with some fruit on the side and ignored the fact that my boyfriend was consuming a cow. I'd learned that if I wanted to keep friendships outside of my vegan circles, I had to let some things go.

But it was really, really hard sometimes.

We settled back with reruns of *The Big Bang Theory* on TV. As soon as Chad took the last bite of his food, he grabbed my hand and tried to scoot me closer. There were two cats, however, between him and me.

He grabbed Freckles—my tabby cat—and set her on the floor and looked at Mr. Mouser. "Another cat, huh?"

"He's just been through a very traumatic loss." I stroked the cat's head.

In the few hours since I'd known Mr. Mouser, he had decided I was his new person. Apparently, the cat was territorial and could only be kind to one person in his life at a time. Thankfully, that was me.

Chad reached for the cat, trying to move him, when Mr. Mouser swatted at him. Chad pulled his hand back and shook it. "Wow. That cat isn't happy."

"He's traumatized," I corrected, rubbing Mr. Mouser's head. "Are you okay? Do you want me to get you a bandage?"

"No, I'll be fine." Chad frowned at Mr. Mouser, who promptly hissed again.

In fact, every time Chad tried to get closer, Mr. Mouser hissed.

Most people thought I was a freak because I loved animals so much, but someone had to look out for these critters.

I'd grown up with two parents who had worked all the time. I'd had a slew of nannies watching out for me. But, as nannies had come and gone, my parents firing most of them for being "inadequate," my cats had remained.

I was the youngest child by far. I had a sister who was twelve years older and a brother ten years older. I was the surprise child who was "gifted" to my parents later in life. They'd already done the childrearing thing, sent my brother and sister to prep school, and were ready to focus on their careers. Then I'd come along and messed up their plans.

They'd never said that. Of course. But actions spoke louder than words. Like the fact that they never had time for me. They checked on me like a doctor might check on a patient after minor surgery—every once in a while, just to ensure progress was being made, and that I was still alive and on target.

One day, while playing in my backyard, I'd found a stray white kitten. I'd named her Snow and fallen in love. I sneaked the cat up to my room, fed her leftovers I slipped into my pocket, and used an old box for kitty litter—I'd convinced one of my nannies to buy some.

My parents were furious when they found Snow. Somehow I'd convinced them to let me keep her. I think the only reason they'd agreed was to teach me responsibility. They'd thought I'd lose interest after a week, but I hadn't. My love had just grown. Eventually, I'd even adopted another kitty that someone at my elementary school had been giving away after her cat had babies.

When no one else had been there for me, my cats had always loved me. During those lonely days of my childhood, my cats had saved me from myself. In return, all I wanted to do was to save them now. Well, to save them and all the other animals that were treated poorly.

"There's something I wanted to ask you, Sierra," Chad started.

I turned to him. "There's actually something I wanted to talk to you about, as well."

"Ladies first." He flipped his hand down, like a gentleman might do in times of old.

I sucked in a deep breath, knowing this wasn't going to go over very well. "Okay. There was a man in my car with a gun after work."

His eyes widened. He shifted to better face me. "What? Are you serious?"

I nodded. "Dead serious."

Bad choice of words.

He reached across the back of the couch until his hand found my neck. He massaged the tight muscles there. "Are you okay?"

"I'm fine. Just a little shaken up." A little shaken up might be an exaggeration. I'd almost gotten into two accidents on the way home. I couldn't shake the feeling of having the gun to my side.

"What happened?"

The whole incident flashed back and I shuddered. "He told me I had to have some kind of information to him by Friday."

"He didn't say what information?"

I shook my head. I'd gone over this a million times in my mind but had come up with nothing. "Nope. I only know it has something to do with Sage."

"Maybe he thought you had information that could implicate him in Sage's death. Maybe someone thinks you know more than you do."

I chewed on my lower lip for a minute. "You're right. That's the only conclusion I can draw also. The problem is, I don't have any of her information."

"Why would someone think you did have it?"

"That's another great question. I don't know. It's not like we were close friends. At best, we were acquaintances." I shrugged. The morbid bottom line remained, though. I frowned as my gaze met Chad's. "He said he'd kill my cats if I didn't get the information."

Chad's forehead wrinkled with worry. "He'd kill your cats? It sounds like it could be someone who knows you well enough to know you love your cats."

I'd thought that exact same thing. The thought wasn't comforting. The man had threatened me not to call the police, told me to close my eyes, and then he'd slipped out of my car. I'd opened my eyes five seconds later, but he was gone. I assumed he'd disappeared into the woods behind the property where the Paws and Fur Balls' office was located.

"You've got to go to the police, Sierra."

The police? Certainly Chad did realize what the implications would be if I did that. "No, I have to find this information. For my cats' sake."

I made a gun with my fingers and pulled the trigger. I knew it was silly. I knew my cats wouldn't understand my words. Still, I couldn't bring myself to voice the thought.

Chad removed his hand from my neck and rubbed his soul patch, just like he always did when he was deep in thought. "How do you plan on finding that information?"

If only I had the answer to that question. But I didn't. "I have no idea. But I'll figure out a way. I always do."

Chad leaned closer. I'd never seen him look so serious. "Sierra, I think this is a bad, bad idea. You're putting yourself in danger."

I didn't care about danger to me. I cared about the danger to my cats. Just the thought of something happening to them made my blood pressure go through the roof. "What else am I supposed to do? Let my cats die?"

"No, but certainly there's a way to keep them safe and to keep you safe. Maybe the police can help you to figure that out."

"I'm not putting my cats on the line." I crossed my arms. I had to show Chad I was serious here. The last thing I needed was for him to be some kind of Lone Ranger and call the police on my behalf. I didn't need any noble gestures like that.

"I'm not suggesting that you put your cats on the line. I'm suggesting that maybe there's a compromise here." He reached for me but Mr. Mouser swatted at him again. Chad frowned. "I don't want anything to happen to you, Sierra."

I didn't want anything to happen to me, either. Someone had to be around to take care of my furry friends. But there were certain risks that came with my job. Apparently, this was one of them. "This is what I do, Chad. I protect animals."

"What about you? Who's going to protect you from danger? Maybe I should call the police for you."

Ah ha! I knew he'd consider doing that. Anger began simmering inside me. I wasn't sure where it came from, but the very idea that I couldn't watch out for myself ignited something in me.

"I don't need someone to protect me! I'm a grown woman who can make her own decisions." My voice started out even but gradually escalated until it was full on blazing with emotion. It wasn't quite as high-pitched as a peacock, but it was getting there.

I told Chad about the man in the car because I trusted him. But now he was trying to tell me what to do. That wasn't cool.

"I know that, Sierra. I know you're very independent. I'm just worried."

Something about the way he said the words brought back visions of my parents and their constant disapproval. I took a deep breath, trying to douse the fire inside me. "Maybe you don't know that. It seems like it's okay for you to put yourself in danger. But I'm trying to stand up for something I believe in and suddenly it's a bad idea."

He shook his head, his eyes dazed. "What are you talking about? When do I put myself in danger?"

Did I really have to spell it out for him? "I don't see you worrying about yourself when you're out there surfing. A shark could eat you, you know. Or you could drown. So many things could go wrong."

"It's different—"

"No, it's not. I think you're being two-faced." I snapped my jaw shut. Where had that come from? My words had surprised me.

Chad stared at me a moment, and his mouth dropped open. "You really think that?"

I kept my chin up. I had to let him know I was serious. The police couldn't be brought into this. "I think you don't understand how important it is that I keep my cats safe. Going to the police is like issuing a death warrant for them. I can't do that. I thought you understood that about me."

"I thought *you* knew *me* better than to think I would do that!"

What? He wasn't making sense! "Animals are my passion. I've dedicated my life to studying them and fighting for them."

Rupert had even said so. He'd said we were cut from the same cloth. Then I remembered that Rupert was single and married to his career.

"Even at the risk of your safety?"

I gave a noncommittal shrug. "There's no other way."

"I don't even know what to say to that." Chad stood and ran a hand through his hair. Finally, he shook his head, his jaw firm and rigid.

A pit formed in my stomach, and I knew this wasn't good. This was the first time we'd ever really fought, and I hated it already.

"I feel like there's nothing else I can say." Chad's gaze connected with mine, almost like he wanted me to blurt something that would make this all better.

I stood there speechless, the definition of a "deer caught in the headlights" of an oncoming break up. I didn't want our night to end this way. But I had to stand my ground. That meant I was on my own.

He dragged his gaze up to the ceiling then back down to me. "I see. I'm going to get going. Maybe some sleep will do both of us good."

"Chad . . ." This was ridiculous. The situation was spiraling out of control, and I didn't know how to fix it. At least, I didn't know how to be true to myself and everything I'd worked toward, while also appeasing Chad.

He paused again, but I didn't know what to say. He stared at me another moment, and I felt like something unspoken was being ascertained by Chad.

Finally, he shook his head, looking dumbfounded, and threw the front door open. Before he stepped outside, he called over his shoulder in an eerily still voice, "Lock up tonight. Please."

I stared at my boyfriend's back as he disappeared from sight. The beads I had over the front door frame clacked in the wake of his departure.

I pulled Mr. Mouser into a hug and stroked his head. What had just happened?

I understood the cat's pain. He'd lost someone he loved. I had a feeling I just had, too.

I couldn't be sure, but all indicators were that Chad and I had just come to an impasse. We'd broken up.

CHAPTER 4

My heart seemed to toss back and forth in perfect cadence with me as I physically flung myself from one side of the bed to the other in a futile effort to sleep.

Usually, the things that kept me awake at night were when I had an important animals rights event coming up. Or when my mind wouldn't leave the horrible facts surrounding an atrocity toward a creature. Or when a brilliant plan formed in the depths of my imagination about how I could open people's eyes to just how cruel and selfish they were concerning animals.

Sometimes, I even lay in bed at night thinking about the book I'd always wanted to write called *Stupid People*.

Those thoughts always got my adrenaline pumping and my mind racing with possibilities.

But right now, I continued to replay my conversation with Chad. How had things gone south so quickly? I still didn't get it. One minute, everything felt normal. The next minute, it was like someone opened all the cages at the zoo and chaos had broken out. It was crazy.

I hadn't even had the chance to tell Chad about Rupert's offer to let me take over as Executive Director at Paws and Fur Balls. Maybe I should just follow Rupert's example and let myself become so busy with my work that relationships were just a fleeting thought.

Why did the idea of that make a rock form in my stomach? Probably because, more than anything, I wanted my life to take a different path than my parents had. They'd been all about their careers. I'd vowed not to follow their example.

Funny, I hadn't even thought about those lonely days of my childhood for a long time. Something about Mr. Mouser had roused the memory from my subconscious. I'd practically been an only child since my siblings were so much older. The only time my parents gave me any attention or showed any type of approval toward me was when my performance matched up with their expectations for me. That's why I'd pushed myself to be an overachiever.

I'd excelled academically and been valedictorian of my class. I'd played bassoon—first chair and made it into a national youth symphony that toured for a summer. I'd been a model student, even getting in my community service hours—at a local hospital, as per my parents' request.

But, all the while, my real passion brewed in my mind. Animals. As you might imagine, this was not the path my parents had chosen for me. Not my dad, a leading oncologist who served on several national boards. Not my mom, a noted pediatrician who was applauded throughout the community for the time she gave to other children. No one knew that she treated other kids with more time and affection than she treated her own daughter.

My sister had become a veterinarian. It wasn't my parent's ideal choice for her, but it sufficed. My brother was a cosmetic surgeon living in New York. Again, my parents would have preferred something a little less flashy.

Then there was me.

An animal rights activist.

Maybe that's why I felt so defeated right now when I thought of Chad. I'd thought he'd loved me for me. But maybe he was just like my parents. Maybe Chad only loved me for who he wanted me to be. He wanted too much control in my life, and that was the very thing I'd always rebelled against.

Just then, from the living room, I heard a slight rustling. Great, was one of the cats destroying a pillow or something? I reached beside me, expecting to find Mr. Mouser. He'd cuddled up beside me and fallen asleep, but now he was gone.

Strange. That cat hadn't left my side since I'd gotten back to my apartment. Maybe the feline had snuck off to get into some trouble.

I was tempted to ignore the sound and just deal with whatever mess had been made in the morning. Then I thought about Mr. Mouser eating the wrong thing, getting sick, and me lying here and doing nothing about it.

With a sigh, I threw the covers off, shoved my glasses on, and swung my legs out of bed. With bleary eyes, I shuffled from my bedroom.

When I walked into the living room, I fully expected to see puffs of cotton or material shredded all over the floor. I thought I might even see my wooden incense holder chewed into pieces or the back of my couch grated and torn.

I paused in the doorway, trying to let things come into focus.

When they finally did, I gasped and shrank back.

There was a man in my living room. Dressed in black. With a ski mask on his face.

The man squatted on the floor, freezing from whatever he was doing, and staring at me.

My eyes fastened on the knife in his hands, wondering if he'd lunge toward me. Wondering if this was how my life would come to an end.

The stare off lingered on and on, each second wrought with tension. I should totally do something, I realized. I just had no idea what.

Instead, I started talking. I had been a debate champion, after all. Maybe I could utilize some of those skills now. Assert my point. Employ reasoning. Offer evidence.

"I have nothing," I started.

He remained frozen.

"No jewelry."

He said nothing.

"I'm broke."

He continued to stare.

"There's nothing here that could possibly be worth going to jail over. See for yourself."

Nothing from him.

Okay, I'd had enough of this. I had to take action. My gaze scanned the room until I spotted my phone on the dining table. Probably six feet away. I just needed to grab it.

Suddenly, the man jostled back into action. He grabbed a black bag from beside him and darted out my front door faster than I could say, "You're barking up the wrong tree."

***

I'd always imagined myself tougher, not the shrinking type. But I'd definitely frozen when I'd seen the man in my apartment. I'd been unable to move for several minutes after he left, even with the phone in my hand. I'd finally realized I needed to call the police. Yes, the police. But I wouldn't mention the mysterious man in my car or the information he requested. Besides, I was calling 911 of my own accord and not because someone else had insisted. There was a difference.

One detective, two officers, and one CSI guy were here now. I had been smart enough to know not to touch anything. They'd taken my statement and now a CSI guy was taking pictures and searching for fingerprints.

"Any idea who the intruder was?" Detective Adams asked. I'd had several encounters with him in the past, thanks to my friend Gabby. He was a middle-aged man of average height with a small soft spot beginning in his belly. He'd always seemed rational and well thought out when I'd met him in the past, which made him okay in my book.

I shook my head. "No idea."

"Anything else you can remember?"

"There is the small detail I should mention that I found a dead body today. You know, just in case that's somehow tied in to this."

The detective stared at me. Why did people always do that?

I filled him in. I lived in Norfolk. The city where I'd found the body was the neighboring suburb of Chesapeake, so the detectives here weren't in the loop.

After Detective Adams got my statement, he paused for a moment. "We'll see what we can do. How's Gabby?"

I remembered my promise to her that I'd keep my mouth shut about her job situation. She hadn't even told her fiancé yet that she'd lost her job with the Medical Examiner and was back to crime scene cleaning.

"Good," I said instead. "She's on vacation."

"Hopefully staying out of trouble. I see you've

picked up where she left off."

    I shrugged. "What can I say?"

    "Be safe, Sierra."

    Finally, they left. That's when I realized I still hadn't seen Mr. Mouser. Most of my other cats had come out and brushed against the officers' legs. Mr. Mouser . . . while he wasn't the most friendly cat, per se, where was he?

    I looked in every room until I finally found him up high in a shelf in my closet.

    I pulled him down and cradled him in my arms. "You knew that man was trouble, didn't you?"

    He purred in response.

    Didn't the officer at Sage's house say he'd found the cat in the closet, as well? Interesting. He must feel safe there.

    As I cradled Mr. Mouser closer, I paused for a moment, contemplating calling Chad and telling him what had happened. Finally, I decided not to. Because he would probably bring this around to an argument about my cats and me choosing their safety over my own. I didn't want to add that stress to the stress I was already feeling. Besides, I wasn't sure where our relationship stood. That realization made a lump form in my throat.

    I glanced at the clock. It was 2:30 a.m., and I was wide-awake.

    I wasn't one to normally snoop unless Gabby initiated it or it involved animals. But since sleep wasn't even on my radar, I went over to my computer and booted it up. I sat back and waited. My computer was so terribly slow. I needed to upgrade, but I couldn't do that until my salary was upgraded. So, instead, I waited and let my thoughts go wherever they wanted.

    It couldn't be a coincidence that someone had

broken into my apartment on the very day I'd found Sage's body, right? The man in my car had made that much clear. But why? What sense did all of this make?

Maybe the intruder had been looking for the video that Chad had taken today. Was there some sort of evidence on the recording that we'd missed? The police had taken a copy, but we still had the original. They'd asked us not to release it to the media, and we'd agreed.

Chad and I had watched the news tonight before our fight, and the station had announced that a woman had been found in the Great Dismal Swamp. Sage's name hadn't been released to the news outlets yet—I assumed they were still trying to inform her next of kin and other relatives.

I turned my thoughts back to Sage. That police officer at her apartment had said that Sage Williams wasn't my coworker's real name. Despite that, as soon as my Internet came up, I typed her name into the search engine. Sure enough, nothing came up. No social media sites, no past articles on her animal rights efforts, no wedding or award announcements.

Nothing.

It was like Sage Williams had appeared out of thin air.

Maybe she had made up an identity. Why would someone do that? Witness protection, as those police officers had joked? Maybe. Running from the law? You never could tell. Running from someone else? A total possibility. And maybe that person she'd been running from had finally caught up with her.

Now that I thought about it, Sage had never wanted to be interviewed for any of the campaigns we'd organized at Paws and Fur Balls. She'd always gotten Kyla to speak for her and had insisted that her picture not be taken.

I'd assumed she was simply camera shy. But maybe there was more to it. A lot more to it.

Besides, if she was camera shy, why was she making a video of herself on the Hessel's Hairstreak butterfly? What sense did that make?

Unless there was more to it.

If I really wanted to get some answers, I'd have to find out her real name first.

And that might be harder than getting a fast food restaurant to stop serving beef.

Leaning back in the chair, I reviewed what I knew so far. If I were to think like Gabby for a moment, I'd have to consider who might have means, motive, and opportunity. I was just brushing the surface of this—and I'd only play detective in my head, mind you. I wasn't going to go out searching for answers or questioning people. I wasn't that crazy.

Sage had been arguing with Donnie. I couldn't imagine what it was about. Donnie seemed too laid-back; he liked everyone. I'd never even heard him raise his voice, unless he was at a protest. He mainly stuck with campaigns where he could play a quiet role.

I could go back to my original theory. Maybe Sage had simply walked in on a drug deal gone bad. Maybe she'd been at the wrong place at the wrong time. But—then why was her apartment ransacked?

I turned off my computer. It didn't matter.

Other than the fact that someone had broken into both my car and apartment, it didn't matter, that is.

Maybe that was unrelated to Sage.

I had a hard time believing it. But it could be true.

I thought of the man who'd broken into my home. Why would he have done that? And what was in his bag? I didn't have anything of value in my apartment. Someone had obviously been to Sage's apartment, as well. But why?

I sighed, stood, and then began checking all of my windows—apparently, that was how the intruder had gotten in. There was evidence he'd used a crow bar and prodded his way in through one of the living room windows. Then I double-checked my locks and laid on my couch, desperate to find—no, not answers—but sleep.

CHAPTER 5

This hardly ever happened. In fact, I couldn't remember the last time it *had* happened. But as I tried to hand out meat-free hot dogs at a local outdoor art show, my heart wasn't into it.

The day was a typical August day in Virginia. Humidity and sunshine mingled, making the day feel even hotter than it actually was. This show, which was running all week, took place at a park with plenty of trees for shade, which offered a slight reprieve. Artists from all over the Mid-Atlantic region were displaying their work in little tents here. The show's director was a friend of Rupert's—and a vegan—and that's how we'd gotten in.

Usually when I was at events like this, I told myself: Just one convert. Just one person to show interest in bypassing meat products. Just one soul interested in leaving this world a better place. Then I'd be satisfied. I would have done my job and feel content.

Right now, as sweat trickled down my back and with my water bottle empty, I thought about Chad. He called me every morning on his way to work. Except today. He hadn't called me today.

He really was mad about my cats. And I think that meant that we really had broken up.

The fact that I felt sad about it was purely ridiculous. I was Sierra Nakamura. I was independent. Top of my class at Yale. A crusader for animals. Content to live—even embrace—the single life.

What I wasn't was a sappy, lovesick woman who depended on men.

No, that title went to other women who had nothing better to do with their lives than make a man happy. That sounded like a miserable existence.

Then why did I feel miserable right now?

"Ma'am?"

I came back to reality, realizing that a college-aged boy was standing in front of me, asking me some question. "What was that?"

"These hot dogs are pretty good. Do all vegan products taste this good?"

I set aside my other thoughts and tried to answer him the best I could. I handed him some literature, another hot dog, and then he walked away a happy possibility.

"Hey, Sierra. I'm supposed to take over for you at noon. I'm a little early."

I looked up and saw none other than Donnie standing there.

"Perfect," I muttered.

He leaned against the table with his arms crossed, looking totally at ease. He wore shorts and a T-shirt and dark curly hair protruded from every opening—his collar, his sleeves, and the bottom of his shorts. At once, I had the image of a capuchin perched in a tree, waiting for the rest of his family group to return.

"How's it been going today?" he asked.

I tried to rewind my thoughts and focus on something other than Chad. "I've had a few people who seemed interested in some information. They took the literature and such. A couple of people have been rude, but we're used to that, right?"

"Unfortunately. I don't know why people think it's okay to discriminate against us. Intolerance . . . when will people ever modify their ways of doing things?"

"For real." It was only okay to discriminate against people who were overweight and animal rights activists. That's how it felt sometimes.

"Any idea why Rupert was at the office yesterday?" Donnie still lounged against our table, in a chatty mood today.

I shook my water bottle, wishing I'd brought another one. I didn't even see a fountain where I could fill it up again. "Doing his biannual check in, I guess."

"I heard he just flew in on Sunday night from Morocco. Must be nice, right?"

I couldn't even imagine having the funds to do that. I barely had the money to support my vegan lifestyle. "I guess that's what you can do when you're a successful entrepreneur. I believe that's the word of the moment."

"How many companies has he started? Like ten? He's never been married. He's filthy rich."

I had the impression from the way Donnie spoke that he held Rupert on a pedestal. "Do we know any of that for a fact?"

Donnie gave me a look that clearly showed he thought I was ignorant if I didn't hold Rupert in as high esteem as he did. "That he's rich? He owns ten companies. How can he not be rich?"

I shrugged, not really in the mood to debate Rupert or his lifestyle. "I don't know. He's very mysterious. What do we really know about him?"

"Just that he reformed himself from acts of domestic terrorism back in the 70s where he used to try to blow up companies that did animal testing? He served his time and now he's more passionate than ever."

Saying it like that made Rupert seem like an urban legend of sorts, at least in my circles. "For the record, he never hurt anyone, and he's since said he regretted his actions. He prefers the peaceful to the violent."

I nibbled on my bottom lip and thought about the offer Rupert had made to me yesterday. I loved the idea of being in charge, especially since I got frustrated when people weren't on the ball with their assignments. But I wasn't sure I wanted to embrace the politics of being in charge.

"I heard Rupert wants to get rid of Bryan."

I tensed, yet tried to look chill. "Bryan has been acting off lately."

"I heard Kyla wants the job."

I raised my eyebrows. "Really? I'm not sure I could see her as the head honcho, but what do I know?"

I knew I might quit if she was in charge. I liked her enough as a coworker, but as my boss? She was way too catty for that.

A moment of silence fell between Donnie and me. I remembered Kyla said something about Donnie and Sage arguing. Maybe I could get the scoop on that right now, especially since the opportunity had presented itself.

"So," I started, trying to keep my voice casual. "What do you think about Sage?"

"Sad. She was a nice girl." He shook his head mournfully. "Do they think it was an accident? Like, maybe she fell or was attacked by a bear or something?"

"I heard she might have been murdered." Why else would the police have been at her place? I reasoned. I could use my deductive reasoning skills here and assume the obvious.

Besides, from what I'd seen, her injuries must have

been small but deadly. A gunshot wound maybe? Her body had been swollen by the time we'd found her and nature had begun feeding on her. That was to be expected. If a bear had attacked her, I would expect more blood, for her body to be ripped apart.

"Yeah, it looks like murder to me. Scary, right?" I said.

"Who would have done something like that to someone as sweet as Sage?"

Sweet? That's not exactly how I would describe her. Irresponsible? Maybe. Flighty? Yep. Unpredictable? Definitely.

Every once in a while, I thought I'd caught a glimpse of pain in her eyes, as well. I had no idea what her past was or how she'd ended up at Paws and Fur Balls. She wasn't exactly the most open person.

From the way Donnie had talked about her, it made me wonder if he had a crush on her. He seemed a little more distraught right now than I expected.

"Your guess is as good as mine. I have no idea."

I told myself I wasn't going to ask questions. But when opportunities like this presented themselves, how could I say no? "I heard the two of you were arguing the other day. That seems out of character."

His bushy eyebrows arched upward. "You heard that?"

I nodded. "I'm not trying to be nosy or anything. I just thought it was weird. I mean, especially because she was so . . ." I cleared my throat. "Sweet and all. And you're so laid-back."

"Yeah, it was odd, to say the least. Sage got all weird on me."

"What do you mean?"

"I went over to ask her a question. She was on the

phone, but I didn't realize that until I reached her desk—her hair had blocked the phone from my sight. Anyway, when she realized I was there, she lashed out at me. Said I'd been eavesdropping and that I should mind my own business."

"Ouch."

"Ouch is right. I've always tried to be nice to Sage, even when Elaina and Bryan got mad at her that time. Remember that?"

Did I remember? Sure, I did. They thought she'd taken over their project and that she needed to stick to her assignments.

Donnie continued. "I stuck up for her. So, when she snapped at me, I kind of lashed back. I shouldn't have."

"What happened then?"

"We went our own ways. A few hours later, Sage came over and apologized. She said she'd been tightly wound lately. Something about she had a lot going on in her life."

"Did she say what?"

He shook his head. "Nope, not a word. I didn't ask. I was happy to put the argument behind us. You know me well enough to know that I'm a make love, not war kind of guy."

I pushed my glasses up higher on my nose. The sun caused a very unflattering sweat to sprinkle across my nose, which made my glasses want to slide down. My parents wanted me to have surgery so I wouldn't have to wear glasses anymore, but I still wasn't comfortable with someone operating on my eyes simply for cosmetic reasons.

"What about the conversation you overheard Sage having? Did she say anything weird?"

"Just something about some money," Donnie said.

"She sounded very stressed."

Money? Were debtors tracking her? Did she have a secret gambling problem? Or was there something more sinister going on here?

Again, I had no idea. I tried to tell myself that I didn't care.

Then I remembered seeing her dead body in the swamp. I remembered her poor cat that had no one now. Well, no one except for me.

I glanced at my watch and saw the time. "Okay, listen, I should run. I've got paperwork to do. I'm trying to finish up this puppy mill story."

"All right. I'll catch you back at the office."

As I walked back toward my car, I couldn't stop thinking about our conversation. Money . . . money could bring about all kinds of trouble.

What kind of trouble had it brought Sage?

***

"We've got to figure out how to handle this," Bryan started. He leaned against the table on his fists. His eyes were wide and intense as his gaze met each of ours. The man could at best be described as passionate, and at worst as temperamental and hot headed. "We can't handle bad publicity."

We all sat around in the conference room, discussing the effect of Sage's death on the nonprofit. Kyla, our public relations girl, took notes.

"The media hasn't released Sage's name yet, so we're in the clear now," I said. I tapped my pen against my notepad, hating these weekly meetings. We spent too much time on useless things like finances and not enough time trying to figure out solutions to the problems of animal suffering at the hands of humans.

"It's only a matter of time," Bryan insisted.

"I don't see how this will be bad PR for us," I continued. "Our company has nothing to do with her death. It's tragic. If the news media comes around, we should all say kind things about her and talk about how she'll be missed. But unless Paws and Fur Balls directly has a link with her death, I think that all of this fuss is about nothing."

Bryan ignored me and turned to Kyla. "Kyla, I want you to have some press releases written up. I want them ready for when Sage's name is released."

"Got it," she responded.

"And if, by some crazy chance, Sage was killed because she was an animal rights activist, we've got to milk it for all it's worth."

"Must you use 'milk it'?" I started. "That expression stands for everything we're against."

"It's an expression!" Bryan insisted, throwing his hands up. "Anyway, I just want to stay on top of this. No one talks to the media without going through me first, understand?"

Everyone nodded. Except me. My brain was too busy going at full speed.

Bryan seemed to notice because his laser vision focused solely on me. "And Sierra, whatever you do, don't leak the video. You can't see Sage on it, can you?"

I shrugged. "I don't know. I haven't looked at it."

Everyone was so concerned with that video. I needed to ask Chad for a copy, just in case. But that would require talking to Chad again. I wasn't sure I was up for that.

I was ready to change the subject. "Where's Rupert? Why isn't he in on this discussion?" I asked. I would think the company CEO would want to stick around to help handle this situation.

"He had to fly out to Chicago about another one of his companies," Kyla said.

He hadn't stuck around for long. He'd been in town for a little more than twenty-four hours. Of course, that sounded like Rupert.

"In other business," Bryan turned toward me again. "How's the puppy mill story?"

"Wrapping it up now," I responded. "I've got everything I need and I can turn this information over to animal control."

"Perfect." He tossed me something.

I caught it in one hand and stared at a . . . collar. "What's this?"

"Your next assignment. It's a shock collar. It's a cruel and unusual punishment that masks itself as a dog training method. I need you to do your research on this specific company. I've heard their collars are even more effective than the competitors, but I've also heard it's because the shock is more powerful. I need you to work on it."

I nodded and put the collar in my purse. "Got it. Anyone know what Sage was working on? Besides the Hessel's Hairstreak butterfly?"

Bryan looked at a sheet in his hands. "No, I'm not sure. She'd told me there was some kind of top-secret investigation. She was really excited about it and asked me to trust her."

Since when had Bryan ever trusted anyone? I kept the question silent and instead asked, "Has anyone searched her desk or computer for information?"

"The police came in and took everything like that," Donnie added. "So that leaves us right back where we were. We don't know exactly what she was doing."

Interesting. Why was she keeping one of her assignments a secret? I mean, Sage liked to be private. But I'd assumed that Bryan, at least, would know some details.

"We have other things to worry about for the time being," Bryan insisted. "Our funding is down and if we don't get more donors, we're all going to be taking a pay cut. That just won't work for me. I'm already giving too much money to my soon-to-be ex-wife as part of this divorce."

So Bryan *was* getting divorced. That would explain some of his behavior recently. Did he have any clue that he could lose his job? Then what would he do to support his wife? I hoped he had a Plan B because even if I didn't take the job, someone else might. I'd hate to see him fall on hard times even more than he was experiencing now.

As the meeting continued, I sat back and observed everyone. There was Bryan. He was in his mid-thirties. Cranky lately. On the brink of doing himself in.

Then there was Donnie. Mr. Laid-back. Did he have a secret crush on Sage? Maybe.

Kyla, the gossip queen, was sharp. She didn't let much get by her. She could handle herself like a pro in front of reporters.

It was an interesting group of coworkers. What would it be like to take over this company and lead this group as Executive Director?

I could be to animal activism what monks and priests were to religion. I could dedicate my life to it. I could be married to the cause.

Except, thanks to Chad, I'd experienced what it was like to love and be loved. I'd tasted that sweet fruit and now I craved more.

My heart sagged.

It didn't matter. Chad wasn't speaking to me anyway. He'd never accept me just as I was.

Would anyone?

***

After work, I decided to swing by Sage's apartment.

All day, my soul had felt unsettled. It was partly over the whole finding a dead body thing and the subsequent intrusion into my house. But, most of all, if I were to be honest, my unrest was because of Chad. Honestly, I missed him.

The two of us were opposites. There was no doubt about that. Our relationship had been a surprise for the both of us.

I wasn't even looking for a relationship. Nope, it was the last thing on my mind. And, if I did ever get seriously involved with someone, I had always assumed it would be with another animal rights activist. After all, I had tons of things in common with people who shared my passion.

But then Chad happened. He'd expanded my worldview, pulled me out of my deeply focused existence, and reminded me that there was life outside of protests and online petitions and eviscerating exposés.

But that wasn't even why I liked hanging out with Chad. No, Chad just made me feel like I could walk on air. He made me feel like . . . well, to put it into cat terms, like I'd found my person.

I'd thought I'd been in love one other time in my life. But that boyfriend—we'd dated in college—had been someone logical, someone I'd made sense with. His name had been Greg, and he was also Japanese, an intellectual, and studious. He understood my upbringing, my strict parents, and the expectations for my future. We could have had a nice life together—a respectable life, just as my parents wanted.

But, the truth was, I didn't want my life to be neat and tidy and respectable. I didn't want to follow in my parents' footsteps. I had no desire to be admired by thousands of people in the community while being despised in my own home. I didn't want to treat strangers better than I treated my family.

Besides, the medical field wasn't for me. My passion didn't lie with healing people, and life was too short to live for other people's expectations. I wanted to pursue my own dreams for my future, even if that meant disappointing people who'd helped to mold me.

Greg and I had been pals, which is a good way to start a relationship. But, in truth, it didn't go beyond that. I didn't dream about being with him. I didn't get flutters in my stomach when he was around. I didn't look at our future together and feel an indescribable excitement.

We'd gotten along fine, though. We never fought. I even converted him to veganism—though it was more for health reasons than animal welfare. Still, I'd take what I could get.

We dated for a year and had talked about marriage, though I never did get a ring. That was just as well. Everyone thought for sure that a proposal was coming. Even me.

But then he'd accepted a medical residency in Cleveland. We didn't see each other for weeks at a time. And I'd realized that I didn't miss him. When we talked the next time he came home, we both had come to the same realization. We didn't want to be with someone we could merely live with. We wanted to be with someone we couldn't live without. And that wasn't the case with us.

When we'd broken up, it had felt like a relief. I felt anything but relieved by this change in my relationship with Chad, though.

I moaned as I wove through traffic. Why did I feel so miserable right now? Then I knew. It was because love could make you feel like this. At least, when love went wrong it felt like this. The emotion was bipolar like that.

Was I being too stubborn? Should I compromise more? Was I going about this whole relationship thing the wrong way?

Probably. How could I be so great at intellectual pursuits yet so terrible at love? I seemed to be better at reading a dog's body language than I did interpreting my own boyfriend's unspoken messages.

On second thought, maybe my expectations were too high. I'd always set lofty goals for myself. I had gotten that trait from my parents. There were certain things handed down to me that I could leave behind—behaviors, recipes for *onigiri*, and anything related to anime. But there were other qualities—ingrained qualities—that were harder. Things like loyalty, respect, and basic temperament.

Maybe the very things I tried so desperately to leave behind were working against me now. After all, you could take a chicken out of a chicken house but it would still be a chicken. Maybe I was fighting myself and purposefully ruining every relationship because I knew that deep down inside me, ingrained within my DNA, I was just like my parents.

I sighed and pulled up to Sage's place. I'd see if anyone had come into town yet to take care of her things—her possessions, her funeral, her body. Then I'd ask about Mr. Mouser.

I tapped on her door. A moment later, a young

woman—probably my age—pulled the door open. Her eyes were red, and she had a tissue in her hands. "Can I help you?"

"You have to be Sage's sister. You look just alike." The woman had the same dark hair, round face, and big eyes as my former coworker.

I watched her expression when I said her sister's name.

"Sage?" She nodded and fluttered a hand through the air. "Right. I am Sage's sister. I'm Thyme. My parents had a twisted sense of humor and named us both after herbs."

I looked down at my empty hands. I usually didn't care about proper formalities. They were just one of the things about my upbringing that I could easily shake off, my secret way of rebelling and showing I was my own person. But there were times—like now—that I wished I did give more heed to those traditions. "I should have brought something. Food. Tissues. A card of condolence."

"Don't worry about it. What can I do for you?"

I glanced behind her at Sage's apartment. Yesterday, it had been a mess. Today, it looked straight and neat. Thyme had been a very busy lady.

"I'm a friend of Sage's. We worked together. I just wanted to let you know that I have Sage's cat. I wanted to make sure he was taken care of in the midst of all this craziness. I didn't know if you wanted me to bring him over or not."

Just at the mention of a cat, she sneezed. "I'm allergic. Please don't. I've been sneezing since I stepped foot into this apartment."

"It's just terrible what happened." I paused solemnly, trying to weigh my words. "I hate to be nosy, but are there other family members who might want the cat?"

Thyme shrugged. "Mom will be here later. I doubt she wants a cat. I guess we'll probably end up taking him to the pound."

A moment of silence passed, and I congratulated myself for not saying something inappropriate at the mention of the word "pound." "I'm sure I can find a home for him, if you need me to."

I'd keep him myself before I took him to the pound.

"I might have to take you up on that offer." She nodded behind her. "If there's nothing else, I have a lot to do. I'm meeting with the funeral home tomorrow to start planning her . . ." She shrugged. "You know."

Her funeral, I filled in.

This would be a good time to go. Instead, I found myself saying, "Listen, I'm the one who found your sister. I haven't been able to get everything out of my mind. Are the police closing in on any suspects?"

She sniffled. "Not that I know of."

"Not to sound insensitive, but do the police know what happened?"

"There was a single gunshot wound to her heart." She shook her head. "I still can't believe something like this has happened. I'm not sure why bad things always happen to my sister."

Now *that* was an interesting statement. "She was unlucky?" Maybe Thyme needed someone to talk to. After all, she was here all alone after her sister had just died.

Thyme offered a half groan, half laugh. "You could say that. From big things in life, to small things. Nothing ever seemed to go her way. And now it all ends like this." She shook her head. "She deserved better. She deserved happiness."

"I'm really sorry. Is there anything I can do?"

"Tell people she was a good person."

I licked my lips, weighing my next thought. Though there were many people who didn't care for Sage, I didn't want Thyme to know that. "Of course she's a good person. I can't believe anyone would say otherwise."

"Exactly. You know she wouldn't hurt a flea. The things that people have said about her . . . especially after her husband died." She covered her mouth. "She probably didn't talk about that part of her life, did she? She wanted to keep so much private. Of course, it doesn't matter now. She's dead." A small sob escaped and she stared off into space.

I dove in, though I'd had no clue the woman had been married. I was fishing for the truth—in my life, this was the only kind of fishing that was acceptable. "That was just awful. Quite the ordeal."

Thyme's eyes widened. "She actually talked to you about it? I didn't think she would tell anyone around here what happened. She was so desperate for a fresh start, for people not to judge her. I guess it doesn't matter anymore. Now this."

I wanted to ask more, but Thyme's cell phone rang. She glanced down. "I've got to take this. It's my mom. I'll make sure and ask her about the cat. I don't have high hopes, though."

She waved goodbye and shut the door.

I stood there for a moment until I owned up to the fact that I had absolutely no idea where to go from here.

CHAPTER 6

I checked my phone again as I walked to my car. It was past eight, and Chad still hadn't called.

I hated the fact that I cared about the fact that Chad hadn't called.

I sighed, refusing to call him. He was the one who needed to apologize. For me to say I was sorry about trying to protect my cats would be the ultimate betrayal to them.

My parents always said my stubbornness would either get me everywhere in life or it would get me nowhere. I didn't want to hear anyone's opinion on what choice this one might be.

It was dark outside already. Another day gone, I mused to myself as I unlocked my car.

I hated thinking about returning to my apartment with nothing to do. I'd gotten used to Chad being there to hang out.

At least I had my cats. But, I had to admit, my cats . . . well, they weren't Chad.

When did I turn into such a sap? When had the change in my life occurred from where people won over cats? I mean, cats gave me unconditional love. They never gave me ultimatums. They always had time for me. They beat people any day . . . didn't they?

I checked my backseat, saw no one was there, and then climbed into my car and cranked the engine.

That's when I spotted the paper on my windshield.

Apprehension rose in me. I had a feeling this wasn't a flyer from a pizza joint.

I looked around for a telltale sign that someone was watching me. When I saw no one and no sign of danger, I opened the door and reached for the paper. I quickly darted back inside and locked my doors.

With trembling hands, I opened the envelope.

The message was simple and clear.

I'M STILL WAITING. REMEMBER YOUR POOR KITTIES. THEY'LL BE CRYING OUT FOR YOUR HELP AND YOU'LL BE POWERLESS TO DO ANYTHING.

Below the sick message was a picture of my cats, taken from one of my social media sites. Each of their faces had an "X" over it.

I gasped and stared in horror at my beloved cats. The sense of danger and urgency increased twofold. I couldn't let anything happen to my babies.

This guy was serious. I couldn't waste any time. I had to figure out how to keep my cats safe.

***

I had to swallow my pride. A lot of my pride.

In my whole entire life, I didn't think I'd ever asked a man for help. I may have paid a man to help me with something—a handyman, that is. And I felt okay about that, because I'd paid for it, so in essence I'd done it myself.

But as I drove through town and pulled up at Chad's bayside apartment, I knew I was stepping into unfamiliar territory. I was . . . desperate.

I stared at the building in front of me. It was right on the shores of the Chesapeake Bay, in an area called Chick's Beach. The Chesapeake Bay Bridge Tunnel jutted out from the middle of it. To the north, there was a view of the resort beach with its high-rise hotels, and to the south there was a military base. On good days, you could see the SEALs practicing exercises out over the water.

Chad lived in a vinyl siding covered transitional style structure that had six apartments inside, each with a balcony that looked out over the water. It was perfect for my beach loving boyfriend—or ex-boyfriend. I still wasn't sure what we were, and that realization pressed down on me.

We'd enjoyed many walks on these shores. We'd talked about life, about the future, about going snorkeling in Mexico one day. We'd made plans and blocked out the other concerns of life, even if just for a moment. We'd even discussed, if we were to ever get married, how many kids we'd want, how we'd balance our schedules, what holidays we'd celebrate, and what our families would think of each other.

How could things have gone south so quickly?

Right now, I climbed the outdoor stairway and pounded on Chad's door, continuously looking over my shoulder for a sign someone had followed me. After all, that's the only way they could have left that note when I was at Sage's. All I spotted behind me was the darkness.

The smell of salty air and rotting sea life filled the atmosphere. Most people didn't think of the smell as dead creatures—it was probably better that they didn't—but that's exactly what it was. Crabs, fish, seaweed, conch egg sacks, jellyfish . . . all of it washed up on shore and created the odor we affectionately thought of as "the beach."

Chad opened the door, and the sound of the TV blaring from his living room floated out. It sounded like some kind of recap of a surfing championship.

He stood there, his eyes narrow at first and then

widening. "Sierra?"

My first impulse was to frown, put my hands on my hips, and let him know just how dissatisfied I was with his controlling behavior yesterday. But I needed his help, and acting like that wouldn't get me very far, nor would it bring any restoration to our relationship.

"Can we talk?" I asked. I shoved my hands into my pockets, hating the awkwardness between us.

He looked over his shoulder. Fidgeted.

I looked beyond him. At the table by his front door. That's when I saw another set of keys there.

"You have someone here?" My mind instantly went to images of a woman. Chad had a woman here? My mouth dropped open.

Maybe I didn't understand Chad, at all. I'd thought he was a good guy. But had he moved on this quickly? Had I meant nothing to him at all?

"I do. But it's not what—"

Just then, Pastor Randy—Gabby always called him Pastor Shaggy because he resembled the character from Scooby Doo—appeared around the corner. "I thought I recognized your voice. How are you, Sierra?"

I glanced at Chad, hoping he saw the questions in my eyes. Since when did Chad and Pastor Randy hang out?

"I'm okay," I finally said. "Been better." I didn't bother to hide the agitation in my voice.

"Listen, it was fun, Chad. Let's talk again some other time." Pastor Randy grabbed his keys and squeezed past me. "I'll see you around, Sierra."

I waited until the pastor was out of earshot before turning back to Chad. "Pastor Randy?"

Chad shrugged. He wore an ugly surfing T-shirt and old khaki shorts that were frayed at the ends. "We'd been talking about surfing together for a while. It turned out today was a good day."

"There are conveniences to being unattached." Okay, so I'd said I wouldn't be hostile. But, here I was, being very hostile. "I'm sorry. I didn't mean that."

"It's not like that." He gave me "that" look. The one that said he was losing his patience and that he felt like arguing would be futile.

I licked my lips. "You guys talking religion?"

"Maybe some."

"Been hanging out with Gabby too long?"

"I'm not all that excited about religion, but talking about Jesus is pretty cool. I'd like to think He was the type who might catch some waves with me."

Interesting. I didn't ask. I wasn't an atheist. I didn't know what I believed.

My parents were agnostic; their parents were agnostic; and who knew how much farther it actually went back? Generations.

Part of me didn't want to be agnostic just because my parents assumed I would be. Not that that was any reason to get religion. I knew that. Instead, I wavered in this in-between place of not really knowing. I didn't want to rule anything out, nor did I want to embrace any ideologies.

I had moments when I thought believing in God had its appeal, if for no other reason than because I wanted to pave a different path for my life than the one my parents had put before me. I saw how Gabby's life had been changed when she started believing in a higher purpose than herself.

But then I figured God was probably something pretty close to a dictator, just like my parents. He was all about rules. The last thing I needed in my life was more ways to disappoint those who had other ideas for my future.

Besides, how could I believe God was loving if He approved of people eating animals? It might sound trite to some people, but it was important to me.

"Can I come in a minute?"

Chad stepped back. "Of course."

We stared at each other a second. I think I was secretly hoping he might apologize, but he did no such thing. He was probably secretly hoping I'd apologize. And so the dance continued, not unlike the mating ritual of hippos where the male attracted the female by spraying her with his feces.

Finally, I started. "Look, I'm not here about last night. I . . . I need your help, actually."

He raised an eyebrow and crossed his arms. "My help? Please then, by all means, continue." There was a hint of teasing to his voice.

He was driving me mad. Didn't he know that what I really wanted was for him to pull me into a hug and tell me that everything would be okay? That I wanted someone to love me for all of me—bad decisions and all? Didn't he know that I couldn't imagine my life without him?

Apparently not, because he continued to stare and wait.

"Someone broke into my apartment last night," I started.

His arms loosened and concern spread over his face. "What?"

I nodded. "I'm not sure what he was looking for. He ran away."

"Wow. Are you okay?"

I raised my hand, just in case he decided to try and comfort me. No, he'd had his chance. That moment had passed. "I suppose I'm okay."

"He didn't hurt you, did he?"

The concern in his voice nearly broke me. "No. He just stared at me, grabbed his bag, and left."

"His bag? Did he take something?"

I shook my head. "Not that I know of. I couldn't find anything missing."

Chad stepped closer. "Have you turned into Gabby in her absence?"

"It would seem so, now wouldn't it?" I shrugged and frowned. "Anyway, I did call the police about the break in. It only seemed right."

"Did you tell them about the threat?"

I pretended like I didn't see the satisfaction in his eyes. "I didn't. But, at least they know something now."

"Good for you. I'm proud of you for reporting the break in."

Irritation pinched my neck. He thought I'd finally given in and seen things his way. The fact was I had no intentions of putting my cats in harm's way. Still, acting hostile wouldn't win me any points right now.

"What can I do?"

I shouldn't ask. I shouldn't ask. But I asked anyway, "Since you essentially offered: Can I bring my cats over here?"

CHAPTER 7

"Since I 'essentially offered'?" He used air quotes.

I hated it when Chad used air quotes. We hadn't moved past his entryway, and I had little hopes that we would. I was standing in the area normally reserved for salesmen and transactions with people buying things from online classified ads.

"You're serious?" Chad stared at me.

"Of course I'm serious." I swallowed the lump in my throat. "They're in danger."

Chad's shoulders looked even tighter. "Are you sure you don't want to come clean to the police about all of this?"

I locked my jaw for a moment. "I can't. I need to handle this myself."

He ran a hand through his hair, leaving his sun-bleached highlights standing on end. "Sierra, you know I love you. But for someone who prides herself in being logical, you're not using much common sense right now."

All my winning arguments seemed to be losing at the moment. Where was all of that great debate skill when I needed it? Besides, Chad had just said he loved me. Was that a slip? Or did he mean it?

It didn't matter right now. "Come on, Chad. I just need your help. Just this once."

His jaw was set in a firm lock and his normal laid-back surfer attitude seemed to be long gone as he stared into space, saying nothing.

"Believe me, I'd only ask if I were desperate, and I'm desperate now."

He turned and looked behind him at his apartment, as if formulating an answer. "You know I'm not supposed to have cats in my building. If my landlord finds out . . ."

"He won't. They'll be gone before he even knows they were there." I hated to beg, especially when there were much more dignified ways of doing things. "Please, Chad, you know they're like my kids. The thought of something happening to them tears me up inside."

Tension stretched tight between us. Chad stared at me. I stared back, keeping my gaze soft.

Chad's head wobbled back and forth uncertainly. "I don't know."

"Please," I croaked.

His shoulders rose as if tightened. "It's complicated."

"It's temporary."

He didn't say anything. His body just seemed to get stiffer and stiffer. If it got any more rigid, he might look like he had rigor mortis.

I decided to forget what was left of my pride. "Please, Chad. I don't know what else to do. I don't have anyone else to ask."

He shifted, his shoulders relaxing some. He closed his eyes, rubbed his temples, and then his tortured gaze fell on me. "Okay, it's like this. I didn't want to mention it because I wasn't sure how you'd react."

"How I'd react?" That was never a good way to start a conversation. "Okay . . ."

He grimaced. "The truth is that they're spraying for termites this week at my apartment."

I stared at him, waiting for him to continue. "And?"

He stared back. "And I thought you might organize

a protest outside of my building or something."

"A protest?" This conversation wasn't going where I expected. In fact, I almost wanted to laugh. Then I remembered those poor termites.

He sighed. "I know how much you love animals—even insects. I thought if I mentioned it you might hold a demonstration."

"Spraying for bugs is kind of cruel," I conceded. Would I have held a demonstration? I might not have, just because it was Chad's place.

Who was I kidding? I had bigger fish to fry than people spraying for termites.

I nearly slapped myself. *Bigger fish to fry?* My thoughts were getting out of control. Next I'd be fantasizing about ham and cheese omelets or buying a leather jacket.

I licked my lips. "I promise not to organize anything outside of your building." Was that really what all of this hemming and hawing was about?

"Fine," Chad finally said. "But only for a couple of days. I've dealt with this termite guy before. He'll turn me in if he sees the cats here."

Relief filled me in one huge burst. My shoulders slumped and my breath escaped in a quick sigh. "It's a deal. Thank you. I appreciate this."

Chad, on the other hand, didn't look relieved at all. He looked tenser than ever with that hard jaw and those uptight shoulders. "And, for the record, I don't think this is the best idea, and it's not because I'm a chauvinist. It's because I only want what's best for you."

I started to protest.

"I'm not sure how much safer the cats are going to be here, for that matter," Chad continued. "It's not like I'll be here all day guarding them."

"I don't expect you to."

He grabbed his keys and stepped outside. "Let's go."

"You're going with me?" His willingness to go above and beyond floored me.

"You're going to need help with all of those cats, right?"

"I suppose."

"We'll take my van."

"Thanks, Chad." We walked silently toward his restored Vanagon and climbed inside. The silence continued as we started down the road. I tried to formulate something brilliant to say, some way to bridge the gaps, to ease the tension, and to make things right without compromising my life's work.

I settled for, "I guess you're still mad."

"Maybe. It's complicated."

I crossed my arms, anger growing in me when I realized he wasn't even trying to mend fences. "Well, I'm still mad, too."

"You're mad?" He looked away from the road long enough to send me an astonished look. "Why are you mad?"

He really didn't know why I was mad? He was not that dense. "You don't understand me. You don't understand how important it is to me that I keep my cats safe. That's basic Sierra 101!"

"That's not what I said! I said—" He stopped as the emotion in his voice rose to the surface. Then he shook his head. "Never mind. You just don't get the position I'm in or know how I feel at the thought of you being in danger."

Sure I did. He probably felt the same way about my safety as I thought about the safety of my cats. He should totally understand my worry and realize that I was responsible for protecting my furry friends. When it came to their safety, the buck stopped at me.

"I think you're the one who doesn't get it. You don't get me." Why did I ever think he would? We were total opposites. Horrible together. A bad idea.

Man, I hated fighting with Chad. But I couldn't bring myself to apologize for not telling the police everything. And he obviously wasn't going to apologize either. That meant that awkward silence stretched between us as he drove to my apartment.

Tears almost—almost—pricked my eyes. I fought them with everything in me. I couldn't let Chad know that he had this much power over me. That would make me weak, and I'd never been weak.

I'd learned to hold my head up high. Like when I got in trouble from my parents for getting an A minus. Or when I skipped a class in college to help rescue some abandoned horses from near death and my professor scolded me in front of the class. Or when my best friend in high school publicly declared me a freak when I started hanging out with the environmental club and writing articles for the prep school newspaper about animal cruelty.

That had been the start of my crusade. From there, a new friend had shown me a video of a dairy farm that had terrible living conditions for their animals. I'd found my purpose in life after that.

I'd started writing letters to my local newspaper. I'd even snuck onto that very farm once and took my own pictures of the cruelty there. Later, I'd organized a boycott. The local news had come out and done a story on me. My passion for standing up for the powerless was born that day.

It seemed to take forever to reach my place, but

finally we did. Neither of us said a word as we walked to my door. I unlocked it, pushed the beads at my doorway aside, and stepped into my living room.

Mittens, Fluffy, Junior, and Mr. Mouser all came out to greet me. I'd been gone almost all day, and they were ready for dinner. Where was Freckles, though?

As I collected some food and bowls and a litter box or two, I called for Freckles. She never came. It was very strange. Despite that, I continued to work. I found three cat carriers and managed to get the other four cats into them.

I almost hated to speak to Chad, but at this point I had little choice. He stood by the door with his arms crossed and a scowl on his face. He wasn't pleased to be here. He probably wasn't pleased to be with me, for that matter. I was determined not to let that fact hurt me.

"I just need to find Freckles, and we can go," I explained.

I looked in closets, under beds, behind the couch, and on top of the fridge. Freckles was nowhere. And Freckles was that cat that always sat in my lap. This was very unusual.

Or was it?

Things clicked so quickly in my mind that I wanted to scream like a momma hyena that had returned home to discover her baby was gone.

My throat burned as I looked up at Chad. "I know what that man took last night when he broke in."

"What?" Chad asked.

"My cat."

***

"This gives a new meaning to 'catnapping,'" Chad

muttered.

Using the back of my hand, I wiped away a tear that popped out of my eye. "That's not very sensitive."

He stepped closer and put a hand on my shoulder. "You're right. I was just trying to lighten the moment."

"Well, it didn't work. I feel worse than ever."

He squeezed my arm. "I'm really sorry, Sierra."

I nodded, trying to keep myself together. But when Chad pulled me into his arms, I felt my resolve crumbling.

"What are they doing to Freckles right now? Why would they snatch her? The deadline hasn't even passed yet."

"I don't know. I have no ideas even, for that matter."

I could barely breathe as I thought about my feline friend. I only hoped she was safe, that the no-good scoundrel who'd snatched her would honor his promise. But when did no-good scoundrels ever do that?

"We should get the rest of the cats out of here." I stepped back and sucked back the rest of my tears. "The sooner, the better."

He picked up a cat carrier. "You got it."

I was beside myself as we drove back to Chad's place. Even Chad didn't seem to know what to say to cheer me up. Or maybe he feared saying the wrong thing. Either way, he was quiet.

How could I have missed the fact that Freckles had been taken? What kind of cat person was I? I thought for sure that I'd done a count last night and all of my feline friends were there. I'd been so focused on Mr. Mouser that somehow I'd missed Freckles.

It was the shock of the break in. That's what it had to be. The normal me, in my typical state, would have never missed the disappearance of a cat.

Still, I felt ashamed. Embarrassed. If any of my animal rights friends found out about this . . . I shook my head. I couldn't stand the thought of it.

We pulled to a stop in front of his apartment. "Here we are," Chad started.

"Yep, here we are."

"Sierra—"

"We should get inside—"

We both started at the same time. I paused and stared at Chad a moment, hoping he'd continue. Instead, he said, "You're right. Let's get them inside before they go stir crazy."

I helped him carry the cats into his apartment and then set up the food and water bowls, as well as the litter boxes. I stroked their heads, whispered sweet words of comfort, and silently begged them to be on their best behavior.

"You want to sit for a minute?" Chad asked when I was done.

"If you don't mind. And just for a minute." I could use a moment to collect myself.

I lowered myself onto his couch, a piece of furniture I knew well from movie marathons and lots of long talks. Right now, I felt like I was sitting on the couch at a doctor's office, waiting to receive a life-changing diagnosis.

Chad sat beside me, looking much more at ease as he leaned back and stretched his arm across the back. "So, what's going on with Sage?"

I shrugged. "Beats me. I haven't heard anything— anything that leads to answers, at least." Which reminded me . . . "Speaking of which, can I see your phone?"

"My phone?"

I nodded. "I want to see the video you were taking

when we found her."

He reached into his back pocket. "I guess."

I took the phone and hit a few buttons until the video popped up. My image came onto the screen. I watched the feed, scrutinized myself as I adjusted my button-up shirt and pushed a hair behind my ear.

On the screen, I smiled at the camera in all of my pint-sized splendor. Really, I'd smiled at Chad, though. The day had started out so fun before it spiraled into a morbid two-day duet of fighting and thinking about death and kitty killers.

"You're the best boyfriend ever," I muttered on the phone. My voice sounded tinny and canned.

"Remember that," Chad had joked in return.

Shortly after that, the heat and bugs had gotten the best of both of us and we'd begun bickering. The thing was, until we'd found Sage dead, we'd really gotten along pretty well. Things had torpedoed out of control until they'd reached the point they were at today.

Right now, Chad scooted closer and leaned beside me to better see the video. He smelled like sunscreen and the ocean, and, for once, that thought didn't make me think of dead fish. It seemed familiar and comforting and . . . all Chad. I often forgot that he used to be a suit-and-tie mortician. He'd discovered that kind of career wasn't for him, though, and gotten out before the rest of his life passed him by.

"You look good on video, you know," he muttered to me.

My throat tightened, and I simultaneously wished he was sitting closer and farther away. "Thanks."

"You really think there's something on this recording?"

I shrugged, forcing myself to look away from his

tantalizing gaze. "I have no idea. I just know that someone's desperate, that they have unfinished work and somehow I've been pulled into this." That thought had me as nervous as a cat in a room full of rocking chairs.

At the edge of the screen, I could see Sage. Of course, at the time I hadn't realized that it was Sage. Nor had I realized that the awful stench I'd smelled was something other than the stench of the swamp.

"I just assumed it was drugs that she'd been killed over. A typical wrong place at the wrong time scenario," Chad muttered.

I nodded. "Me, too. But too many other things aren't adding up. There's obviously more to it. I just don't know what."

Though initially I'd wondered if this video was the information demanded from me, after watching it, I had to disregard that theory. There was nothing incriminating here.

So someone was searching for some other kind of information. I had no idea what. I only knew the lives of my cats were dependent on me finding it.

"What else do you know?" Chad asked.

I told him about what I'd overheard the police officers say about Sage not being her real name, her sister's revelation that Sage had been married before, and the top secret investigations Sage had been engaged in on work time.

"Sounds very mysterious," Chad said.

"I know, right? I had no desire to get involved. I wanted to mind my own business, and now look at me! Someone broke into my house and into my car. Whether I like it or not, I'm involved."

Chad squeezed my hand, and my heart softened a moment. Maybe everything would be okay between us. I desperately wanted things to be back to normal and, for the first time since all of this had happened, I felt hope that might be possible.

Chad shifted. "Hear me out for a moment. Please. Sierra, I really think that if it's the cats someone wants, maybe you should hand them over."

I sucked in a quick breath and pulled my hand away. "What?"

"Let me finish." He raised his hands as if to protect himself from a verbal assault. "Hand them over to someone else who can take care of them for a while. Maybe even someone out of state and far away. It's only a matter of time before someone realizes that the cats are here."

"But at least I can see them here." The thought of being far away from my cats pained me, causing a physical jolt through my heart. "Besides, who do I know out of state?"

"You won't be able to see them at all if something happens to them." He shrugged. "I know this isn't what you want to hear, but how about your parents?"

Indignation rushed through me, along with outrage, disgust, and mortification. "My parents? Are you crazy?"

"Sierra—"

My mind was already racing, along with my emotions. "My cats will be little orphans in that house by themselves with no one to care for them! I might as well set them out to roam the streets and fend for themselves. Plus, that would require talking to my parents."

"Sierra—"

"My cats are like my children." The words continued gushing out. Bringing up my parents had ignited something in me, some kind of protectiveness. I didn't want anyone else—human or feline—to experience the kind of upbringing I had. "What kind of person would I be if I sent them away? Besides, I don't think these threats have anything to do with my cats except for the fact that they're using them as a bargaining chip. If my cats weren't in the picture, they'd probably just go straight for my jugular."

"Sierra, I didn't mean it like—"

I stood before I got any more emotional. We hadn't mended any fences at all, had we? I kept picturing my cats with my parents and my emotional train wasn't just derailing, it was imploding. "You know what? I can't talk anymore."

"But—" Chad reached for me, then let his arms drop to his side.

I wasn't sure which option he'd raised was worse: the police or my parents. But both suggestions had freaked me out, pulled me away from any of the thought out logic I prided myself in. "I should go. As soon as I can find a safer place for my cats, I'll take them off your hands. I'm sorry to put you out of your way."

Before he could say anything else, I left.

I successfully managed to make it to my car before I started crying.

CHAPTER 8

I stayed in Gabby's apartment for the night. She'd given me a spare key, and it seemed safer to stay there than my own place. Unfortunately, I didn't get any sleep.

As I'd lain in bed, my thoughts haunted me. Thoughts of Chad. Thoughts of my cats. Thoughts of the mysterious "information" the man had requested.

What was this information? Where would I find it?

When I'd woken up, I had a plan. Perhaps not a good plan, but a plan nonetheless.

I hadn't wanted to get involved in all of this. Really, I hadn't. And I had no experience tracking down criminals—other than puppy mill owners—but I figured I knew enough about cats and their methods of hunting for prey that I could utilize some of their skills.

Cats were programmed from birth to chase, born with an instinct for hunting. They honed those skills at a young age through playing. Cats learned to gage distance by pouncing. They learned to adjust their speed to the speed of moving objects. They learned to be patient, to wait until just the right moment to reveal themselves. They learned to watch the objects of their mealtime affections and observe their movements, their patterns, their way of doing things.

I was going to have to utilize some of those very skills. I'd watch. I'd wait. Then I'd pounce.

I went into work early the next morning and arrived before anyone else got there. I went to Sage's desk and rifled through her things. I knew most of her stuff here was work related. A couple of grants, some project ideas, etc.

I found what I was looking for beneath the plastic sectioned organizer in her small drawer. It was a key.

I'd once overheard Sage saying she put it here. There were advantages to having a small office space and little privacy at the workplace. Tidbits like that, for example.

I grabbed the key now, left a note for Bryan telling him I was working on the puppy mill exposé, and then slipped out. The puppy mill excuse wasn't quite the truth, but maybe while I was out I would try to work on that story. I put in enough extra hours—unpaid, at that—that I could miss a couple of hours without feeling guilty.

I went back to Sage's apartment complex and sat outside. Just as I hoped, I saw Thyme leave thirty minutes later. I remembered her saying she had to make funeral arrangements today. I didn't want to capitalize on her loss, but the time was now to look for whatever it was I needed to save my cats.

My cats were like my children. I would do anything for them. Even this.

Before I got out of my car, my phone rang. I looked down at the number on the screen and scowled. It was Chad. I almost ignored it, figuring he'd have some other absurd idea on how I should run my life. But then I remembered he had my cats. I had to make sure they were okay.

"Hello," I answered.

"Hey, Sierra." I could tell by his voice that he was being cautious and restrained.

"What's going on?" I would keep myself aloof until I heard what he had to say.

"I thought you'd want to know that your cat cried all night for you."

Sadness pressed in on me. "What?"

"Mr. Mouser. He let out the saddest sound I've ever heard for half of the night. I didn't know cats could sound like that."

"What happened the other half of the night?"

"He gave up on thinking you were coming for him, so he shredded my couch instead."

A rock formed in my stomach. "Really?"

"This Mr. Mouser is a bit of a feline terrorist. I know it's not what you want to hear. He's kind of scary, though."

"Not scary. He's just scared." I had to force the words out. "I'll pay you back for your couch."

I wasn't sure how, but I would. Somehow. Someway. If it was the last thing I did. A headache began pounding at the back of my head.

"Listen, I'm not all that worried about my couch. But I am exhausted from not getting any sleep. Have you thought about boarding the cats at a local kennel? I know it's expensive, but I can help with the costs. I just can't have another night like last night."

"Chad—" How could I convince him that was a terrible, terrible idea? Why? Because they'd be in a cage all afternoon without hardly any attention. They'd be without me. They'd feel lost and alone and abandoned.

Kind of like I felt as a child.

"Yes?" Chad finally said.

"I'll see what I can do," I finally answered.

I knew Chad had a lot riding on him this week with Gabby being out of town. His job was physically demanding, and he needed his sleep.

Still, I wished Chad could bear with the cats for just

a few more days. Part of me thought Chad just wanted to make me realize that in order to keep me safe, the cats needed to be far away. The other part of me thought this was some kind of power struggle, and he secretly wanted me to choose between him and my cats. How could I have ever thought I had a future with this man? My emotions had steered me in a totally incorrect direction, and now my heart had to deal with the aftermath.

"Just to let you know, I'm locking Mr. Mouser in the bathroom—if I can grab him without having him take my hands off. I'm convinced he's part lion. A better name for him might be Mr. I'll-Kill-Anyone-Within-One-Foot-of-Me. There's nothing mousy about him."

Alarm spread through me. "Don't hurt him."

Chad sighed. "You know me better than that, Sierra. Have I ever hurt an animal?"

"Lately, I'm just thinking I don't know you at all! I thought you liked me—all of me—just as I am."

Now why had I said that? I did know Chad better than that. He was kind. I'd always felt safe with him. When things were good between us, he made me feel like I could win wars.

"Sierra, I do like you for you."

"If you're even thinking of putting my cats in danger, then you don't get me. I'm sorry, Chad, but I have to do this. I will try to find a better place for my cats, and I'll pay you back for your couch."

Right now, my time was ticking away. I had to get inside that apartment. I had to admit I desperately wanted to end this conversation, as well.

"I've got to go." With that, I hit the END button.

My heart felt heavier and heavier with each conversation Chad and I had. It was like watching a beautiful sandcastle crumble in a storm and knowing you couldn't save it. Or even worse—you could save it, but you knew allowing it to crumble was for the best.

I climbed from my car and walked down the sidewalk like I knew what I was doing, keeping my head high and my steps even. As I got closer to Sage's door, I reached into my pocket and pulled the key out. I checked quickly to make sure no one else was around before sliding the key into the lock and slipping inside my friend's apartment.

I'd never done something like this before, and my heart was racing. If I were caught, I'd be in so much trouble. That wouldn't be a good thing. I mean, it was one thing to get arrested at a protest for animals. I might even be okay with being charged with breaking and entering at an animal testing facility. But not for breaking into someone's home. That was just creepy.

I had to work quickly.

I stared at the space around me. It wasn't anything fancy. In front of me was a great room with a breakfast bar separating the kitchen from the living area. The apartment was light and airy with sunlit carpet and monotone white and beige decorations.

Moving fast, I crossed the room to the desk I saw on the opposite side. This would be a great place to start, I figured.

Just as I began looking through the files on top, my hand accidentally hit the crystal vase there. It started falling to the floor. I tried to grab it. But it was too late. The vase hit the side of the desk and shattered.

Red drops hit the carpet. I was bleeding.

My blood was on the white carpet.

Panic filled me. I had to get that up. Now.

The last thing I needed was for my DNA to be found here. For all I knew, my DNA was already on file in some kind of criminal database due to the bombing several months ago where I was the prime suspect. Thankfully, I'd been cleared and the real culprit had been arrested. Still, I wouldn't put it past the feds to have collected some of the hair from my brush in order to match me with evidence at the scene.

And I'd been the one to find Sage's body.

This wasn't going to look good.

Quickly, I grabbed some paper towels, wet them with warm water, and began blotting the spot. Only part of the blood came up. I could still see some spots.

I went to the bathroom, rummaged around until I found some ammonia, and then poured some of that onto the carpet.

I could still see red.

What was I going to do?

I pulled out my cell phone and called Gabby. She'd know how to get the blood up.

So would Chad for that matter, but I wasn't speaking to him at the moment.

I really hoped she would answer. And she did. Hearing my friend's voice brought me a surprising joy. "Gabby! You answered! What's going on?"

"I'm just sitting here, wearing this fancy fur coat at this luxurious resort. They're giving furs out because, you know, everyone here is rich and all. Maybe you should come and stop them."

"Ha ha. Very funny." I paused, considering for a moment the fact that she might not be joking. "But if anything of that sort happens, let me know. I'll be right there."

"I don't doubt it. How are you and Chad doing?"

"I don't want to talk about it," I insisted. I picked up a few more pieces of the vase and stuffed them into the first place I could find—my purse. Already, in the back of my mind, I knew this was a bad idea.

"That doesn't sound good."

I sighed, realizing I was bleeding again. I grabbed some more paper towels—I'd brought the entire roll over at this point—and wrapped them around my hand. "We had this huge fight. I really don't want to get into it over the phone."

"I'm sorry."

I had to concentrate on the task at hand. "Quick question before I forget. What's the best way to get blood out of carpet?"

"Are you serious?"

"Yeah, unfortunately." I stared at the blood on the carpet. Another drop dripped onto the floor. I had to treat my cut. It was deeper than I wanted to admit.

"Are you in trouble?"

"I'm fine. I'm just doing a little . . . undercover work. Puppy mill stuff." Oh no. Another little white lie. But I didn't want Gabby to worry. She deserved to have some fun. "But the blood is human, not dog, so don't get sad or anything. I'd ask Chad but I'm not speaking to him right now."

"Okay . . . is the blood dry or fresh?"

Another drop escaped my makeshift bandage and landed on the carpet. I frowned. "Definitely fresh."

"Use cold water. Mix some hand soap with some water and blot it."

"I tried that already."

"You can use some ammonia."

"Tried that, too."

"Why don't you just go to my apartment and grab some of my cleaning solution?"

"I was hoping you'd say that. Thanks!"

"Are you sure there's nothing you want to tell me? Chad's alive, right?"

"Very funny. He's fine. I'll fill you in when you get back. Anyway, how about you? How's it going at Allendale Acres? You and Riley been practicing that scene with the song 'Love Is Strange'?" I stuffed some more dirty paper towels in my purse and then grabbed a handful of clean ones so I could continue to blot.

"No 'Love Is Strange' reenactments." Gabby filled me in on a missing person there at the resort where she was staying.

I sighed. "Oh, Gabby. It's no mystery that these kind of capers find you."

"Tell me about it. There's this small problem that Riley asked me not to get involved."

Why did I feel like I could relate to that all too well right now? Hearing Gabby talk caused a well of emotions to rise up in me. Mostly anger at Chad. Maybe at men in general.

I took a break from getting the blood up, waiting a moment to see if more blood would tinge the carpet as the liquid dried. Instead, I looked through some more papers on Sage's desk as we talked. I knew my time was limited, and that I should keep this conversation short and sweet. Still, it felt really good to talk to my best friend.

"Oh, no. Does he know that you can't help yourself?" I saw a whole bunch of papers and receipts that didn't help me one bit. Was all of this searching in vain? I could go to jail for this! For an animal, I might make the sacrifice. That's what I had to remember. My cats were worth this.

"No, not yet. He's been distracted with his conference."

"You've got to tell him. You know that, right? For

that matter, I think you should tell him that it is highly insensitive of him to even ask you not to snoop." Men, I mentally snorted. They all wanted you to change.

"Insensitive?"

"It's like asking you not to be you." Just like Chad was asking me not to be myself when it came to my cats. Loser. My feline friends never asked me to change. That was just one more reason they were so great.

"I thought you liked Riley."

"I love Riley. And you two together are like Sonny and Cher." It was true. They were perfect.

"They got divorced."

Who else could I compare them to? "Okay, how about Romeo and Juliet."

"They died."

"Fred and Wilma Flintstone?" *Lame, Sierra.* "Anyway, I think you're perfect together. But you shouldn't have to try and be someone you're not." Again, just like Chad and my cats.

"It's called compromise. And it's just for a week."

I had to snap out of it. I was in a terrible mood. "You know what? It doesn't matter. I'm just in a rotten mood, and I've got to get the blood out of the carpet."

We chatted for a few more minutes. Then I realized I had to hurry through the rest of this conversation. I had a mission. We said goodbye, and a new sense of urgency filled me. I had to get this blood cleaned up. I squatted on the floor, trying to dab up more evidence that I'd been here.

I ran into the kitchen, searched for some bleach, and then dropped some onto the floor. The blood started to disappear. It wasn't ideal, but I wasn't sure if I'd be able to get back here again to do a better job. I had to be careful, though. The smell of the bleach was strong. If I used too much, it would be a sure sign I'd been here.

As I squatted on the floor, I spotted something on the bottom of the desk. I paused for a moment and stared at the triangle of paper that stuck out from behind some drawers.

I reached forward and pulled the paper out.

It was an email that had been printed out. And maybe it was my first real clue in my search for a way to save Freckles.

CHAPTER 9

The email was from someone named Tom. He said he was going to be in town—I double-checked the date—this week, and he asked if he could meet Sage, despite everything that had happened in the past. Better yet . . . they were supposed to meet today at a hotel down at the beach.

Who exactly was Tom? Why had he emailed Sage? It had been important enough that she'd printed out his email. In my experience, you only printed emails if you had a good reason.

The CSI techs had been out here, but somehow they'd missed this paper. Probably because it had slipped out the back of the drawer and into the recess space behind it. I would have missed it if I hadn't been squatting on the floor like this.

I peered up at the desk and saw a couple of other things sticking out. This was obviously the police's loss but my gain. Gently, I prodded the papers down. The first was a Post-it note with the name Eileen and a phone number. Interesting.

Important? It was hard to say. But, either way, I wanted to hang on to it.

The second piece of paper was written on familiar letterhead from Paws and Fur Balls. I read the words there. "Sage, I have two tickets for the ballet this weekend. Would you like to go with me?"

Who was this from? Donnie? Maybe the man really

was interested in Sage, as more than just friends.

Unrequited love could lead to a myriad of sins and obsessions and fatal mistakes.

That's what all the detective shows on TV seemed to hint at, at least.

Just then, I heard a lock click. Panic raced through me.

Was Thyme back? Already? This wasn't good. I didn't have time to hide. Not to really hide.

I quickly stashed the Clorox behind a plant, threw the rest of the paper towels into my purse, and darted under the desk. It wasn't the best hiding space. Not by a long shot. But it beat sitting out in the middle of the apartment.

Voices carried in from outside. A door rattled. How would I ever explain this one? Even worse—how could I protect my cats if I was in jail? I couldn't. If the killer didn't get to them, Chad just might send them to kitty jail, otherwise known as "The Pound." Even more horrifying was the thought that he might send them to my parents.

Then the sound outside the door faded.

Her neighbors, I realized. That must have been one of her neighbors getting home.

My heart rate slowed. A little.

The moment had made me realize I had to hurry. This kind of investigating wasn't my thing.

I kept the papers, stuffing them in my pocket. Then I cleaned up any evidence that I'd been here. You could hardly tell I'd bled on the floor. I took the broken vase, put it in a bag, and then stuffed it all in my purse while mumbling silent apologies to Sage, as if she was alive and here listening to me.

As a last minute thought, I pulled a potted plant over the space. This would do. For now, at least. If I had the opportunity, I'd come back with Gabby's industrial strength chemicals.

Right now, I had just enough time to get to the oceanfront and meet this Tom guy.

Of course, if he'd killed Sage, he probably wouldn't show.

If he'd heard she was dead, he probably wouldn't show.

But, for the lives of my cats, I had to try.

Because, unlike the saying, cats really didn't have nine lives.

***

I walked into the lobby of one of the swankiest hotels at the oceanfront and glanced around. I hadn't had time to do any research, so I had no idea who I was searching for or what this Tom guy looked like. Mostly, I saw tourists in bathing suits, loaded down with boogie boards and sand pails headed out to the beach.

Nor had I any time to get cleaned up. I still squeezed a paper towel in my hand. The bleeding had stopped, until I reached into my purse for my keys and grabbed a piece of broken glass and added another cut to my collection.

I'd stopped by a fast food restaurant—the only time I ever frequented the places—and washed my hands. Then I disposed of the paper towels and all of the glass I could scrounge up. There were still bits and pieces that I'd need to get out later.

After about ten minutes of trying to look inconspicuous while standing near the display advertising different tourist attractions, I spotted a thin balding man wearing a golf shirt and khakis sitting on the couch, glancing at his watch. He wasn't dressed for the beach, nor did he have a family hovering close by. No, it was like he was waiting to meet someone. Sage, maybe?

I lingered for a minute, waiting to see if anyone would show. When no one did, I took my first step his way, wishing I had a better cover story. Wishing I had any cover story, for that matter.

"Tom?"

He looked up, surprise marring his gaze. "Yes?"

"I'm Sierra. I'm a friend of Sage's."

"Sage?" He laughed, the sound tight with rigidity. He stood and hiked up his belt. "Nice to meet you, Sierra."

"Same here."

He glanced behind me. "Is Sage coming?" He said "Sage" with a touch of bitterness.

I stared at him, trying to determine if he was putting on a show. Did he really not know that she was dead? From what I could see, he had no idea the woman had been murdered.

Then I had a horrible thought. What if Sage had been running from someone? Like that whole witness protection theory the police had joked about? What if I'd just admitted to some psychopath that she lived here?

Of course, Sage was dead now, so it probably didn't matter, other than the fact that I could have just inserted myself into something ugly. Besides, what were the chances she had more than one person who wanted to kill her?

"I'm afraid Sage can't be here," I finally said.

The hopeful expression slipped from his face as he sunk down into the chair. "Oh. I see."

I sat across from him, studying his expression

carefully and wondering how to approach this conversation. Before I could start, he dove in. "Why did she send you? Are you a lawyer?" His face clouded at the word "lawyer."

I shook my head.

"A mediator?"

I shook my head again.

"Come on, make this a little easier on me. Who are you then?"

"I'm a friend. Sage couldn't be here. I knew she wouldn't want to miss talking with you, though." I decided to see if he would take the bait, all the while knowing I could be playing a dangerous game.

He raised his eyebrows. "Did she tell you that?"

I tried not to cringe or have any telltale sign of my deception. "Not in so many words."

"What did she tell you then?"

"That you were an important part of her life." I took a guess. "And that she wished things had worked out differently. She had regrets about the past, also."

Maybe this was her ex-husband. An ex-boyfriend? A lover who'd broken up her marriage?

I just couldn't get a feel for Sage's relationship with this man.

"I see. Well, I'm real sorry about the way things went down between us," he continued, his voice pulling tightly. "It's taken me more time than I would like to realize that."

What in the world was he talking about?

"She was confused about why you wanted to see her," I ventured. "She's being very cautious. I'm sure you understand."

"I wanted to say I'm sorry. To say I finally understood and believed in her. To see if we could have a clean slate." He glanced at me. "I'm probably asking for too much, aren't I?"

I shook my head, nothing making sense still. "You never know unless you ask."

He frowned. "Since she sent you, I guess that means there's no chance Sage will meet with me while I'm in town?"

I shook my head, measuring my words carefully. "Look, I know this will sound weird, but she never did say exactly how you knew her. She just said she couldn't make it and asked if I'd come in her place."

He looked sharply at me, as if the question surprised him. "She didn't tell you about our relationship? I can't believe that. I thought she'd take every opportunity to shred me apart."

"Which means?"

He was definitely an ex. I'd bet my kitty litter on it.

He twisted his lips in a half frown. "It means she's my stepmom."

CHAPTER 10

I pictured young, twenty-something Sage. Then I looked at forty-something Tom, and a very strange family picture formed in my mind.

Knowing that they were related, I came clean about what had happened. I explained to Tom that I had to know for sure I could trust him before sharing that news and apologized for my ruse.

Either Tom was a great actor or he'd truly had no idea she was dead. He claimed his family hadn't watched the news all week, that they'd been trying to unplug and spend quality time together while here on vacation.

"The police don't know who did it?" he asked.

I shrugged. "Not that I'm aware of."

"Who are you again?" His eyebrows wrinkled together.

"I'm a friend of hers from work. I found the email from you, and I wondered if she had some unfinished business." I shrugged. "I was just trying to help out, since Sage couldn't be here herself. I didn't want you to hear about this through the grapevine."

"I tell you what. I gave Ani—I mean, Sage, a hard time. I really thought she'd only married my dad for his money."

So, her husband had been rich! That could cause some problems.

"But when he died, she gave all of his money to charity. Which may have proven that she wasn't after his money, but initially it made me equally as mad. That money should have been mine."

The mystery just continued to deepen. Sage was married to an older, rich man who'd died and left her a hefty sum of money. I had trouble picturing this alter ego of Sage's, though. Nothing about her screamed rich or privileged or gold digger.

I needed more information. "Why the change of heart? What made you decide to give your stepmom another chance?"

"I realized that money was making me miserable. It might sound crazy, but I realized that I have enough. I'm a successful businessman, and it feels good to have earned my money myself." He shook his head. "You want to know the whole truth?"

I nodded. Duh. Of course!

"My friend won the lottery. Sounds great, huh? But after he won, his life fell to pieces. Everyone wanted a piece of what he had. He ended up divorced. Two of his kids aren't speaking to him. It was just terrible. That's when I realized that not getting the money may have been the biggest blessing of all."

I remembered that Donnie said he'd heard Sage arguing with someone about money. With one of her stepchildren maybe? Tom?

"Is that what your brothers and sisters think too? That they're okay without the money?"

He shrugged. "I'm not sure. I haven't talked to them in a while."

"Can you think of anyone who'd want to hurt Sage?"

"To hurt her? Plenty of people. Back in Montana, people still think she killed my father."

I gulped. Killed? There was so much more to this

story than I thought. "But she didn't take his money. What other motive could she have?"

"Maybe she was just sick."

I shifted as I sensed the hostility in his words. This man was saying one thing, but his body language said another. Perhaps he'd been the one in my car, begging for information on . . . Sage's money? "When did you get into town, Tom?"

"Saturday. I'm on vacation with my family."

I wondered when Sage's exact time of death was. I'd never heard, which made it hard to draw any conclusions. I did know that she'd gone out on Friday to film the segment, however. "Have you guys been at the beach the whole time?"

"Everything we need is right here." He spread his hands out as if to indicate the tourist strip in Virginia Beach. "Restaurants, mini-golf, fun houses. Most of all—the beach." He held up some tickets in his hands. "Even get to see your local baseball team play on Thursday. My son is a fanatic, so we're going for him. Just picked up the tickets from the concierge."

"So, you're saying you didn't see Sage at all on your trip?"

He leaned closer, his nostrils beginning to flare. "What are you suggesting?"

"I'm just trying to rule you out as a suspect." I stood my ground, not looking away from his intense stare.

His face reddened. "I am not capable of murder."

I raised my eyebrows. I'd bet that was what a lot of killers said.

***

My only regret from my conversation with Tom

was that I hadn't found out Sage's real name. He obviously knew what it was. That's why he'd made a face when he'd said, "Sage."

But after I'd nearly accused him of killing her, I couldn't exactly go back and ask for a favor. *By the way, what was her real name again? You don't want to share that? How about you just tell me your last name? I could take that and run also.*

That was okay, though. Because I had another plan, one that I thought was quite brilliant.

I stopped by Chad's apartment—he wasn't home, but I had a key—and picked up Mr. Mouser. I then swung by a nearby vet who I'd worked with in the past. I really hoped she could help me. I asked the receptionist if Dr. Maxwell had a moment for me. A moment later, a perky blonde with short hair appeared from the hallway.

"Hey, Meg!" I knew the veterinarian shared my love of animals. She'd helped me out more than once before. In return, I always tried to send potential patients her way. It was a win–win for both of us.

She and her husband ran the clinic themselves and often didn't charge clients who couldn't afford the vet bills. Her husband also worked at a local humane society to help cover their bills here at the clinic.

"Hey, Sierra. Who do you have here?"

I propped the carrier on the counter. "I have a homeless tabby that I've taken in for the past couple of days. I'm hoping you can help me to identify the owner."

"Is he micro-chipped?"

"I hope so."

It was devious. I knew it was. But this cat should be registered. If he was, then I might be able to find out Sage's real name.

If I knew Sage's real name, I might be able to figure

out why someone was trying to hunt her down. Then, in turn, I might be able to find the elusive "information" the man in my backseat had requested and save my own cats.

"Let's see." She reached to get Mr. Mouser, but the cat swatted at her and hissed. She frowned and shook her head in disapproval. "You're not a happy camper, are you?"

"Let me get him for you." I took Mr. Mouser out of the carrier with no problem. I really didn't know why so many people had issues with this cat. He seemed fine to me.

Meg waved me into the back. I ignored the scowls from the three other people in the waiting room and hurried toward the exam rooms. There, Meg pulled out a scanner and ran it over Mr. Mouser's back.

Microchips were wondrous things. No bigger than a grain of rice, they contained a radio frequency identification transponder that was encapsulated in bioglass. The device stored unique ID numbers that were saved in an animal recovery database for times just like this.

Well, kind of for times like this.

Meg stepped back, scribbled something on some paper, and handed it to me. "I've got the registration number. Talk to Annie, the receptionist. She can look it up for you and tell you who the owner is. You want us to call his people?"

"I've got this one. You guys already have enough to do. Besides, I feel kind of attached to this guy."

"Speaking of which, how's 'the boy'?" That's what she called Chad. Probably because he was the only man I'd ever spoken of in the five or so years since I'd known her.

I shrugged. "It's complicated." I glanced at my happily married friend. "Meg, would you ever want to be with someone who didn't love your cats as much as you did?"

She didn't hesitate before answering. "If someone didn't love my cats, I'd know they weren't the love of my life," she said.

Her words only made my heart heavier. I forced a smile. "Thanks."

"Of course, love is never, ever easy. I'm probably not being much help, am I?"

"No, you have good insight. I appreciate it."

Back at the desk, Annie hopped on the computer. As she typed it in, I tried to put Meg's words out of my mind. But did she have a point? Maybe Chad and I were truly incompatible. Maybe I'd just been in denial.

Or was I reading too much into this? Maybe Chad wasn't trying to control me at all. Maybe, just maybe, every time I got close to people, I started thinking they were like my parents.

"Here you go." The receptionist slid a piece of paper toward me.

I stared at the name there. Finally, I had my information.

And it was a whammy.

This cat belonged to Anise Wentworth.

Even *I* had heard of that woman before.

CHAPTER 11

Before I'd left, I asked Annie if I could board Mr. Mouser there until I connected with the owner. I explained that I'd pay for the expenses in the meantime. Annie had told me their kennel was booked all week since many of her clients were on vacation.

Despite our differences, I wanted to remain respectful to Chad. He wanted the cats gone, so I tried to honor his request. I called two more friends. One had just gotten a new dog that hated cats. The other was about to go out of town.

I briefly thought about taking Mr. Mouser back to my apartment. Then I remembered the threat that had been made to all of my cats. They were better off somewhere else, somewhere they'd be harder to track down.

For that reason, I mentally apologized to Chad.

Then I dropped the cat back off at his place. Just for a little while longer until I could find someone else. I'd promised by the end of the day.

While I was there, I'd seen Chad's couch. Mr. Mouser truly had destroyed it. His sharp, cat claws had shredded the sides. Guilt pressed in on me. I was going to have to find the money to repay Chad. I just didn't know how.

Finally, I went into work and plopped into my desk chair. Plopping wasn't like me, but I was exhausted. Thankfully, only a few people were in the office. The rest were down at the fishing pier posing as dead fish in order to send a message to everyone around that sea creatures were still animals.

"How's the puppy mill exposé coming?" someone asked behind me.

I swallowed back guilt and turned to see Donnie standing there. "I'm closing in." I did have almost all the information I needed. I just had to compile it and turn it over to the authorities. I had high hopes they'd shut this breeder down for good.

"Good for you. Whenever profit is more important than the well being of a dog, it's an atrocity." He leaned against his desk, ready to talk. "Speaking of atrocities, the police were in here again today."

That made me perk. I turned to face him better. "Really? Why'd they come again?"

"Still investigating Sage's murder. I guess they wanted to see if there was anything they missed the first time."

My mind raced. "And did they find anything?"

He shrugged. "They took Sage's computer."

"Did they say if they had any suspects?"

He twisted his head as if my question surprised him. "You really think they would tell me that?"

I shook my head. "No, not really." I needed a reason why I'd asked that question, and I needed it fast. "I just worry that there's some connection between her death and her work here. I mean, we have to face it. We're not on anyone's 'Most Likable' list."

"I can't argue with that, but I hardly believe someone would kill us over any of our stunts." Donnie studied me. "Who do you think did it?"

I sighed. "I have no idea. I really can't comprehend the concept of anyone justifying taking another human life." I glanced at him, trying to tamp down my eagerness for answers. "How about you? Any ideas?"

He rubbed his chin. "She was working on some undercover investigation. Said she couldn't talk about it until she had more information."

I remembered Bryan sharing that at our meeting. I'd thought it was strange then. I still thought it was strange now. "Weird, since we usually all share our information with each other."

He nodded. "That's what I thought, too. But I guess Bryan approved it. That's all that matters."

Just what was she investigating? It was something worth considering. Her nosiness could have gotten her in trouble. Or maybe I was looking too hard for answers. Maybe the culprit was much more obvious.

I studied Donnie for a moment. I knew he loved animals. I also knew his own cat had died about a month ago from old age.

For a second, I considered asking him to keep my cats for me. But there was still a small part of me that didn't trust him. If he was involved in all of this somehow, I could be leading my cats to their death by asking Donnie to take care of them.

I remembered his resemblance to a certain monkey species. Maybe Donnie and capuchins weren't just similar physically. After all, capuchins had a ritual of crushing millipedes and rubbing their remains on their backs to act as an insect repellant. Had Donnie thrown someone else under the bus in order to save his own skin? I didn't know.

I did have one more question for Donnie. "By the way, do you like the ballet?"

He raised his eyebrows. "I consider myself a modern man. But no, I can't even fake being interested in the ballet. Why?"

I shrugged casually. "Someone here in the office was talking about the last ballet that came to town. I just remember it was a guy, and I'm trying to recall who."

"Probably Bryan. He loves that kind of thing, apparently. I'd check with him."

***

At seven o'clock that night, I was the only one at the office. The only sounds were of the AC blowing through the room and the overhead lights humming. The odor of burnt popcorn—thanks to an incident by Kyla earlier—still lingered in the air. One by one, I'd said goodnight to my coworkers, and they'd scurried home.

I had more than one reason for staying late. First of all, I needed to catch up on things so I didn't lose my job. Plus, the quiet was kind of nice. It beat going home to my empty apartment. I wasn't sure I'd be welcome at Chad's, though being away from my cats was seriously bothering me at the moment. If I were to be honest, being away from Chad was bothering me, too. I had to keep my thoughts occupied with something other than him.

With everyone gone, I did an online search on Anise Wentworth.

Anise Wentworth. I couldn't believe it.

Even I had heard about the trial against her, and I was by no means a news junkie.

As I waited for the search engine results to pop up, I chewed on the fact that I hadn't recognized her, in the least. Her face had been on the news as the trial unfolded. Back then, she'd had blonde hair, a thin build, and an upper class composure.

Between the trial and now, she'd become a woman with curly dark hair. She'd gained some weight and liked to dress in clothing that was loose and flowing. I would have never guessed her to be the trophy wife they'd portrayed at the trial.

My eyes widened, however, when I saw a long list of articles about Anise. I refreshed my memory on the details of the trial against her for the murder of her husband. She'd been found innocent, but some of the details were sketchy.

I read more of the specifics, just out of morbid curiosity, I supposed. What I found especially interesting was the fact that her husband had been forty years older than she was. Forty years. When they'd married, Sage—or Anise—had been 25 and he'd been 65. So, of course, everyone thought she'd married him for his money and then killed him off.

Ernest Wentworth had made his fortune on some wise stock market investments. He'd then grown those investments into an empire. He bought struggling businesses and turned them around. He invested in up-and-coming technology companies.

As far as millionaires went, he remained relatively quiet and out of the spotlight. Everyone had seemed surprised when he'd married Sage. His first wife had died fifteen years earlier to cancer, and he wasn't the skirt chasing type of man. But somehow Sage had won his heart.

Making matters worse, the substance that seemed to have killed him was an overdose of allergy medicine combined with his heart medicine. Sage claimed that she would have never poisoned her husband, that she loved him. She claimed that her husband simply got the pills mixed up, and he had started to show some signs of dementia. He'd done a couple of business deals recently that had him stressed, as well.

Her saving grace during the trial was the fact that she'd been seen that evening at work. She'd been an investigative reporter. That was right! How could I have forgotten that detail? She'd returned home at almost midnight and found her husband dead in their 10,000 square foot house.

I checked the time and location of the trial.

Ernest and Sage had lived as husband and wife in Montana. That was four years ago. Sage had started working for Paws and Fur Balls about eight months ago.

As soon as she'd been cleared of the charges, she must have moved out to this area in order to start fresh. I'd had no idea what her past had been. I wondered if anyone else at the office did? Chances were, if one person knew, they would have told someone else, who would have then told someone else. That was the way office gossip usually worked. Especially if Kyla got ahold of it.

My final question was on why Sage's real identity hadn't been leaked to the news yet? Certainly the police knew. It seemed as if family had all been notified. The media would be all over a news story like this like a dog on a ham bone.

I was still no closer to any answers, but I did have more questions. That was better than nothing.

As I stood and stretched, I heard a tap at the door. My senses all went on high alert. Who was tapping at the office door at this hour?

My first thought, of course, was a killer.

But a killer would have to be pretty stupid to make himself that obvious.

Right?

I peered around the corner and spotted . . . Chad.

And he didn't look happy.

I prepared myself for another confrontation,

another demand that I remove my cats from his property.

But if I felt so mad at him, why did my heart still speed when I saw him? Stupid heart. I guessed I was just one of those stupid people I wanted to write a book about.

I pushed the door open and ushered him inside, locking up behind him. I was still paranoid that someone could be waiting in the shadows to knock me off.

"Where have you been, Sierra?" he demanded.

"What do you mean where have I been?"

"I've been trying to call you all day." His voice sounded even, but restrained.

"Yeah, well, after our last conversation, I didn't exactly want to speak with you."

"Someone is making threats on your life and now is the time when you decide not to answer the phone?" The emotion in his voice escalated with each word.

"I thought you were calling to fuss at me about my cats again." I crossed my arms over my chest.

"I'm not fussing about your cats. I'm fussing because I'm worried about you. I want you to be safe. There is a difference, you know."

"It doesn't feel like there's a difference."

His gaze zeroed in on my hand. "What happened?"

I looked down at my bandages there. I'd stopped by the store and gotten something to cover up my cuts. "Nothing major. I just broke into someone's house, dropped a vase, and the glass cut me."

"Broke into someone's house? Sierra, have you lost your mind?"

"I'm fighting to survive here, Chad. I'm doing whatever I have to."

He sucked in a deep breath and finally shook his head. "Did you even listen to my voicemails?" His eyes were so wide that I could see the white all the way around his irises.

"No. Why would I put myself through that?" Seriously. I'd figured I'd just feel worse afterward. Besides, I was trying to secure a temporary home for the cats before we talked again. I'd had no luck with that.

"You are impossible sometimes," he muttered.

"You're pretty impossible yourself," I muttered back.

He rubbed his jaw. "Listen, the termite guy just left a little while ago. Just as I thought, he told my landlord about the cats, and my landlord came to talk to me about them. They've got to go or I'm going to be kicked out."

I tried to loosen my stance. "I'm trying to find a place to take them. It's harder than you might think."

"I know you're trying, Sierra. But all I have is one more day. That's all I can give you."

One day was better than no days. "Thank you. I appreciate that."

Suddenly, his gaze caught on something across the way. "Is that . . . a litter box?"

"Yes." Why was he acting like he'd never seen one before?

He stormed toward it. Stood there. Stared at it. His hands went to his hips. Then he looked up at me with a stupefied expression on his face. "Why is there a litter box at work?"

"Because some people bring their animals here." As soon as I said the words, I wished I hadn't.

"What? You mean, you could have brought your cats here? I could have avoided this whole confrontation with my landlord?"

Guilt pounded through me. "It's not that simple. Some people bring their dogs. Dogs and cats don't get along that well. It can be quite disastrous at times."

Besides, what if the person threatening my cats was a coworker? I'd be leading my furry friends to their deaths by bringing them here.

He leaned closer. "I wish you'd fight for our relationship like you fought to save animals." Despite the hot emotion in his voice, I heard . . . hurt?

My heart squeezed. "What does that mean?"

"It means that there's only room for one passion in your life, and that passion isn't me." He ran his hand through his hair. Then he looked up and shook his head. "Watch out for yourself tonight, Sierra. Lock your doors. If it's not asking too much, could you text me when you get home so I don't worry all night?"

I think I nodded. I must have because he waved goodbye and left.

I stared at him. I hadn't been slapped. Not physically. But I might as well have been.

I felt numb. In shock. Speechless.

Of course I would fight for Chad.

Then why wasn't I? Why was I letting him walk away right now?

I didn't know.

But I did know that I felt like my heart was breaking in two.

CHAPTER 12

I wasn't sure what got into me because I normally wasn't a violent person.

But, after Chad stormed out, I was aggravated. Really aggravated. So aggravated that I kicked the litter box.

The top came off and granules scattered all over the floor. A foul smell also leaked from the area, and it was obvious the box hadn't been cleaned in a while.

I walked past the mess I'd made there, ignoring it for a moment, as I stomped to my desk. My stomping would have been more effective if pieces of kitty litter hadn't stuck to the bottom of my shoes and deadened the full impact of the sound.

Why were relationships so complicated? If relationships were meant to be, did that mean they should be easy?

I had no idea. Of all the things I'd discussed and debated at Yale, true love wasn't one of them. Too bad.

I had to do something to distract myself. So, I fished the Post It Note out from my purse, nearly cutting myself in the process. I had to get the rest of that broken glass out of my purse. I didn't want to do it here, though, just in case the police came back again and went through our trash. I wanted nothing to tie myself with Sage's place.

I dialed the number for Eileen. A moment later, a woman with a soft, high-pitched voice answered.

"My name is Sierra, and I'm a friend of Sage's."

"Oh, thank goodness you called. I was getting so worried."

"Worried?"

"When Sage didn't show up to meet me, I thought something might have happened. She called last week and said she had an update for me."

"I see." I paused, collecting my thoughts and trying to soften my voice. "Eileen, I'm sorry to be the one to break the news to you, but Sage is dead."

She gasped. "Dead? What in the world? I just talked to her last week."

"I'm sorry. The police found her body on Monday."

"How . . . ? I mean, what . . . ?"

"She was shot."

"That's just terrible. I can't believe this." She sniffled.

I leaned back in my chair, my thoughts churning. "Eileen, maybe I can help you. Does this have to do with her work as an animal rights activist?"

"No, this was a personal investigation she was working on. It did involve animals, though."

Interesting. Maybe this was the project Sage had been so private about. Maybe this was my first real lead. "Listen, Eileen, could we meet in the morning? I'd like to figure out if I can finish the work Sage started."

"Someone needs to finish it. I can't just let this injustice slide past, not when so many others have been affected." She paused. "I'm in town from North Carolina. I'd planned on leaving around lunchtime tomorrow."

"How about we meet at MacArthur Center at 9:30? That's the big mall here in downtown Norfolk. Would that work? The food court should be open."

"Yes, thank you, Sierra. I'm so glad this isn't going to be ignored."

I hung up and stared at the phone a moment. Interesting. Why would Sage be doing a private investigation?

I'd find out in the morning, I supposed.

I stood and stretched. I had to get out of here. Before I left, I needed to clean up the biodegradable kitty litter that now stretched across the floor. Funny, Sage usually did this.

I found a broom and began sweeping up the granules. I threw them away and then picked up the litter box. Some kitty litter remained on the bottom, along with some newspapers. I might as well clean the whole thing out. I carried it over to the trashcan and dumped everything.

A plastic bag at the bottom made me look twice.

There were papers in that bag that had been hidden under kitty litter and newspapers.

Maybe I was finally on to something.

***

My hands were shaking as I sat at my desk. Slowly, carefully, I opened the bag and pulled out a file. What I found there were emails, hand jotted notes, photos, and typed reports. Was this Sage's secret project?

I quickly scanned the file. She was gathering information on a local laboratory called Bernstein and Associates. A lab? That usually meant one thing.

Animal testing. Was Sage doing an exposé on the company? Why hadn't I heard about this before?

I continued reading and saw something about testing on cats. All the information put together didn't make much sense. I couldn't ascertain what kind of testing was being done on cats or for what purpose. The notes seemed scattered and disorganized. Sage had obviously written in some kind of sloppy shorthand that I couldn't interpret.

There were also some interesting pictures. Pictures of a man and woman smiling over dinner. Blackmail pictures? I couldn't be sure.

But there was one name that stood out, that appeared over and over again.
Andre King.

I did a quick Internet search and found his home address. He was a head researcher at Bernstein and Associates, had been quoted on various subjects in different scientific magazines, and he lived in Norfolk.

I added one more person to my list of people to visit tomorrow.

I gripped the file I'd found. Sage had hidden this for a reason.

This *had* to be the information someone was willing to kill for. That meant I had to plan my next move carefully.

"What are you doing here?" someone barked beside me.

I gasped. When I looked up, I saw that Bryan was here. Standing behind me. Scowling.

Who was Sage trying to keep this information hidden from?

I swallowed hard and braced myself for whatever came next.

CHAPTER 13

I lowered the papers and forced a smile. "Just working late."

He glared at me. "On that puppy mill project?"

"Wrapping that up."

"What do you have there?" He stepped closer.

I pulled the papers toward me. "This isn't actually work related."

He continued to eye me suspiciously. "Let me guess. Is it an official offer from Rupert to take over my job?"

I swallowed hard again. I didn't want to own up to anything until I knew his mental state. "Why would you think that?"

His hands went to his hips and he frowned. "Don't you think I know he wants to get rid of me? I figured you'd be the first person he approached."

"You have seemed distracted lately."

He sighed, pulled out a chair, and collapsed into it. "You know my wife left me a few months ago, right?"

I nodded, unsure where this conversation would go. "I did hear that."

"I've been miserable without her."

"Then why did you ask Sage out?"

His eyebrows shot up. "You knew about that?"

"Sage told me," I fibbed.

"I should have never done it. I thought maybe if I went on a date with someone that my wife would get jealous and want to get back with me." He shook his head before letting it hang. "It didn't work. Not only was Sage not interested, but my wife couldn't have cared less."

My heart squeezed for a moment. "I'm sorry."

He sucked in a long, deep breath before releasing it. "Me, too."

I remembered him mumbling something about money during our last staff meeting. I wondered if he was desperate enough for money that he would try and get with Sage, just to get a portion of her late husband's money. If I was going to ask him, now was the time.

I tried to be diplomatic. "Bryan, did you know Sage wasn't Sage's real name?"

His eyes widened. "What are you talking about?"

"Sage was really Anise Wentworth."

"The gold digger?" His mouth gaped open. "No, I watched that trial. They look nothing alike."

"She changed her appearance and her name. I think it had something to do with that undercover investigation she was doing, the one she wouldn't talk about with anyone." I shrugged. "Maybe it had something to do with Paws and Fur Balls."

He scoffed. "I can't believe that."

"Why else would someone who could be a millionaire choose to take on a job like this, one that practically puts its workers at poverty level?"

"Because she loved animals. You can't argue that."

No, I couldn't. Sage did love animals.

"If you're thinking she was investigating me, you can feel free to check our books. We're clear. You can check my bank account too, for that matter. If I wanted to make a lot of money, I wouldn't be working this job. I think we can all agree with that."

I nodded. I believed Bryan. I did.

So who did that leave on my suspect list?

I hoped that after tomorrow, I would have some more answers.

***

I'd almost—almost being the key word—spent the night on the couch in the break room at Paws and Fur Balls. It beat going back to my empty apartment where I could only socialize with my thoughts and feel the emptiness of my furry creatures being gone. It would only remind me that Freckles was in the hands of a sociopath who preyed on innocent people and creatures.

But showering and changing clothes at my office space would be difficult given the fact that there was no shower and I had no clean clothes. Therefore, I'd gone home. Just to be safe, I decided to stay in Gabby's apartment again.

When I got out of the car in the parking lot of my apartment building, I felt like the weight of the world was on my shoulders. Well, I always kind of felt like that, but today the notion was even greater than usual.

I swung by my mailbox, realizing I hadn't checked my mail in a couple of days. I'd had other things on my mind. I saw a thick envelope mixed in with lots of bills and advertisements. My name was written in a rough scrawl on the yellow paper.

Tension filled me. I instinctively knew this had something to do with the mess that had swept into my life this week with the force of a F5 tornado.

With trembling hands, I opened the package. Inside, I saw a collar.

I gasped. This was Freckle's collar. I'd know it anywhere. I'd had it especially made for him by one of my friends. It was hand stitched in yellow with the word "FRECKLES" across it in black letters.

A piece of paper dropped to the ground. I grabbed it before the breeze could carry it away.

The words I read there made me go cold.

"Two days. You have two days to get me the information or your little cat will go to animal heaven." "Heaven" was scratched out and the word "Hell" was written above it. "Consider this your final warning."

***

After a restless night, finally the sun came up and I got ready. I'd hardly slept a wink as I thought about Freckles. I had to think of a way to save her. I'd do whatever it took.

My first order of business for the day was paying a visit to Andre. I left a quick message at Paws and Fur Balls, saying that I'd be working at home for a while.

Then I drove to Andre's house. It was a nice place, all brick and stately looking with an expansive lawn that was well taken care of. There was one car in the driveway, and I hoped that belonged to Andre.

I leaned back into the seat of my car, thinking things through for a moment. What did I have so far?

Andre seemed like my best lead right now. I had pictures of him. Dining with a woman.

I considered the possibility that Sage was trying to blackmail him. Maybe she'd threatened that he had to come clean about some cruel testing he was doing or she'd let the images go public. That seemed like a good reason for murder.

At 8:45, I got out of my car and trudged up the sidewalk. I had the papers I'd found in the litter box in hand—I'd made copies of them first, of course—and I was prepared for a confrontation.

The best I could tell, this was the information my home—and car—invader had requested. I wanted to give it to Andre and know that my cats would be safe. I had a feeling that Andre King was my man, that he had the answers I was looking for.

After he had what he wanted, then maybe I could pick my cats up and maybe—just maybe—Chad and I could have a decent conversation about all of this. I could show him he could be first priority. Maybe he could prove that he wasn't trying to control me.

I pounded on the door. A moment later, a prickly looking man who wore his glasses at the end of his nose and had dark hair long enough that it flipped up at the ends greeted me. "Can I help you?"

"I'm looking for Andre."

"You've found him. Isn't it a little early to be out selling Girl Scout cookies?"

I bit back a sharp retort and instead raised the folder in my hands. "I have the information you want. Now I want Freckles back and I want you to leave the rest of my cats alone."

He blinked. "Excuse me?"

"You heard me." I held up the file folder again. "I have what you want. So you can leave me alone and stop trying to ruin my life."

"I have no idea what you're talking about." He put his hand on his hip and stared at me.

I let out a quick breath to show my disbelief. "Look, I know that Sage was trying to blackmail you. She took pictures of you with a woman. I'm sure you don't want your wife to see the photos."

"My wife? I'm not married."

I shifted, tired of this game. I'd done my practicing, watching and waiting. Now it was time to pounce. "Your girlfriend then."

"I'm not dating anyone."

His response silenced me, but just for a moment. "Then why do you care about pictures with some mystery woman?"

"Exactly! Why do I care? What are you talking about?" His eyes were wide and bulging. His movements—and words—were coming faster.

I pulled out a photo. "This! Isn't this picture what all of this is about? Sage threatened to go public with your sultry behind-the-scenes lifestyle if you didn't stop doing animal testing?"

He stared at the picture a moment and then snorted. "Lady, you're off your rocker. That woman in the picture is my boss. We're having a business meeting. I'm not attracted to the woman but, even if I were, it wouldn't be a crime because she's single also. And who is the Sage woman you keep mentioning?"

My theory was falling apart right before my eyes. "She went by Sage Williams. I have evidence to believe she was doing an exposé on you."

"On me? Why in heaven's name would she do an exposé on me?"

"Because you're doing nefarious things to animals in your lab, that's why!"

"Nefarious? Way to use a new word."

This man was grating on my nerves on so many different levels that it wasn't funny.

Just then, a cat rubbed against his leg. He picked the creature up and cradled her. "I would never hurt an animal."

I flinched. How could someone who treated

animals horribly act so loving toward an animal companion they kept at home? People could be such a contradiction at times. "Then what do you do at your lab? These papers here show you're doing some kind of testing on them."

"We do independent tests on products. The individual test depends on what we've been contracted to do. We test products for the presence of lead, we do chemical analysis, and we also have an allergy lab."

I blinked, trying to mask my confusion. Allergens? Sage's sister was allergic to cats. Did this somehow tie in with Thyme? Why exactly was this top secret then? There didn't seem to be anything sinister about sneezing.

I stuck to my guns, though. "Were you aware that someone was collecting information on you?"

"No, I was not." He put the cat down and crossed his arms.

My theory continued to race toward the edge of the cliff, toward its death. I didn't stop it—I just let it run, hoping something, anything, would save it from certain demise. "Maybe the name Anise rings a bell?"

Something glimmered in his eyes. Recognition? "Anise? Well, yes, I do know Anise."

Bingo! Finally, some of my mojo could safely return home and do a victory dance. Much like a lioness returning to her pride after a successful hunt. I only hoped my hunt didn't end with anyone—or anything—being dead.

"Did you guys have a disagreement?"

"I don't know that I'd call it that." He glanced at his watch. "I really must get to work."

"Were you mad enough to kill her?" I had to at least ask that question before this conversation ended.

"Kill her? Are you insane? Why would I do something like that?"

"Because your business was at stake."

He let out a scoffing sigh. "You're off your rocker. My means of revenge would be a legal one. What can I say? The legal brief is mightier than the sword." He laughed at his own joke. "Look, I didn't kill her. I was helping her."

"Helping her with what?"

"It was twofold. First of all, she was doing an article. If you must know, that picture you have was supposed to run with it."

"Oh." I wasn't nearly as good at this investigating thing as Gabby was. "You knew that the whole time and didn't tell me?"

He smirked. "Secondly, Anise wanted me to test some cat hair and cat dander samples for her."

"What?" I was dumbfounded. Truly.

"You'll have to put the rest of it together, Einstein. I've got to run."

I had a strange feeling he was angry about something. I saw the emotion flash in his eyes. But, before I could ask him, he closed the door.

**

I wrapped up my little confrontation with Andre just in time to make it to the mall and meet Eileen.

I had mixed feelings on Andre's involvement in all of this. He was Sage's little secret project. I had no idea why she would have kept him a secret. The story very well could have been discussed at the office, and we could have brainstormed some ways of nailing down people who were possibly using animals as lab rats.

Only, it didn't appear Andre was using animals as lab rats.

Nothing was making sense.

I drove down to MacArthur Center, an uppity local mall. After leaving my car in the parking garage, I hurried inside and up an escalator.

I saw a woman sitting by herself in the food court. Every few seconds, her gaze scanned everyone around her. I figured she was my girl.

"Eileen?" I asked as I approached.

Her whole body seemed to tense. "Sierra?"

"That's me." I sat across from her.

Eileen was probably in her fifties with frizzy blonde hair, a long face, and a very unflattering fuchsia sweat suit. I hoped I didn't regret meeting with her and that her involvement with Sage could add something to my investigation.

As I sat down across from her, averting my eyes from her sausage biscuit, I forced a polite smile. The woman looked upset. Her eyes were red and her face blotchy.

She wiped her mouth with a crinkly napkin with the name of a fast food joint across it. "Thank you for meeting with me."

"It's no problem."

She took a bite of her breakfast, and I had to look away. That poor, poor pig that had to suffer, just so that people could eat a lousy sausage biscuit.

I leaned forward, trying to put those thoughts aside. "I'm really sorry about Sage. It sounds like she was working on a big project for you."

Eileen nodded. "She was. She'd put months into it."

I shifted, trying to get a better handle on this conversation. "What exactly was she investigating for you?"

"My cat. Her name is Lulu."

"What's wrong with Lulu?" Maybe Sage was

secretly a pet detective. Wouldn't *that* be interesting? I knew a simple answer like "Sage was searching for missing pets" was too easy, though.

Eileen sucked in a deep breath. "I found this man who said he'd developed and bred cats who were hypoallergenic."

Hypoallergenic? That was not where I expected this conversation to go. Did this tie in with Andre and his testing?

"That's nearly impossible," I interrupted, feeling that it was my duty to inform people of their misinformation. "It doesn't matter what anyone says. You'd have to change a cat's basic genetic code in order—"

"I know." She held up her hand, her eyelids droopy as if I'd already exhausted her. "Trust me, do I ever know. But there's this researcher who claimed to have developed one. No matter how crazy it sounded, he had all of this scientific proof to back it up. Said he'd spent millions of dollars on his research. He had experts who supposedly backed him up. I believed him."

"I see." I pushed my glasses up higher.

"Maybe I'm just gullible, but it sounded like a dream come true. I've always wanted a cat, but I was never able to have one. I jumped at the opportunity. I emptied my savings in order to buy one of these cats."

"How much did he charge?"

"Twenty-five grand."

I nearly choked on the air I was breathing. That was outrageous. Especially when considering there were tons of little kitties in the pound who would love a home.

But I had to focus.

That man had preyed on the needs of cat loving yet sneezing prone people. How despicable.

"What does this have to do with Sage?"

"She called me. Said she was doing an exposé on the company. Apparently, there are other people who have been ripped off by this guy. He has this contract that he makes you sign, and it has a lot of fine print. But after talking to him, you'd think he was a god practically. He was very convincing. I really didn't think anything of the contract. That's where he gets people."

"Did you call him afterward?"

"I talked to him once, expressed my concerns, and he promised to get back with me. He never did. When I tried to call him again, his number was disconnected."

"Where is the company based out of?"

"Chicago is where their address is. But he travels to deliver the cats personally, so I've never seen the supposed headquarters."

Chicago? That's where Rupert had a home. He couldn't be . . . I shook my head. No, he couldn't be involved in this. He was an animal lover, not a con artist.

I leaned closer, processing all of this. "How did Sage find you?"

"The newspaper in my hometown had done a story on me. They put it online, and that made me easy to find."

"What's this man's name?"

"Brandon Channel."

It didn't ring any bells with me. "So, what exactly was Sage investigating?"

"She thought Brandon was scamming everyone. She wanted to nail him."

"In other words, your cat still made you sneeze and your eyes water and whatever else happens when your allergies kick in?"

The woman nodded. "That's correct."

"Did you meet him yourself? Can you tell me anything else about him?"

She slowly shook her head before shrugging. "I don't know. He ended up sending an assistant. She was a woman with dark hair, slender, very business-like."

That didn't help to narrow down anyone. Not really. "Did this Brandon guy have any degrees? Anything that qualified him for 'developing' this cat?"

"He worked in veterinary medicine, but he also had a degree in . . . something else. I can't remember what it is right now. His bio sounded very impressive. Now I wonder if any of it was real."

"Did you tell the feds?"

"No. I mean, other people claim that he's telling the truth. Experts have even backed him up, and a couple of vets endorsed him. I thought, at first, that maybe it was just me. Then Sage came forward and I finally felt justified in my concerns."

I thought about my options. This had to tie in with everything . . . didn't it? Otherwise, why had Sage been so secretive about it? "Why don't you let me look into it?"

"Would you?"

I nodded. Why not add one more thing to my list? Besides, at best, this could possibly tie in with Sage's death. At worst, I could add it to my list of projects and really impress Rupert.

At this point, it was anyone's guess what the outcome would be.

CHAPTER 14

I remembered Eileen's description of the woman she'd met. A slender woman with dark hair, very business-like. Could that person have been Thyme? Maybe she'd convinced Ernest Wentworth to invest in this BioCare company so she could profit off the scam? I wasn't really sure at this point. But I wanted to find out. At the very least, maybe Thyme could offer some insight.

The countdown continued to tick away in my head, as well. That note I'd found with Freckle's collar indicated I had to have this information ready to turn over by the end of the day tomorrow. I'd do whatever it took to find what I needed.

That's why I knocked at Sage's apartment door, and Thyme answered a moment later. "Hi, it's Sierra. I stopped by earlier this week."

She nodded behind her. "Of course. Come in."

I stepped inside the apartment, letting the AC wash over me. I couldn't help but quickly glance over at the area where I'd bled on her carpet. From where I stood, it appeared the plant still covered the spot. I let out a mental *whew* and resisted the urge to wipe imaginary sweat from my forehead.

I turned to Thyme. "How are you?"

"Been better." She shrugged, seeming melancholy.

I glanced around the room and saw no evidence that someone else was here. No suitcases or plane tickets or extra sets of car keys. "Where's the rest of the family? I thought they were coming into town."

She lowered herself onto the couch and motioned for me to do the same. I sat in the chair across from her instead and waited for her to continue.

"My brother's in town and so is my mom. That's about it. They're staying at a hotel, though. They said staying here would be too painful. Too many reminders of Sage, you know? I can hardly bring myself to pack up her things." Her gaze met mine again. "What can I do for you?"

"I was wondering if you had an update on the cat? Would you like for me to bring him back over?" *And maybe a few more cats in the meantime until this craziness in my life passes over?* Of course, I didn't say that last part.

"That's right. I know I can't have any animals at my place, not if I want to breathe. Let me check with my brother and mom today. It totally slipped my mind."

"Sure thing. It must be frustrating being allergic to cats, especially since your sister loved them so much."

She shrugged. "Cats have never been my thing. My sister was the one who went crazy over them."

"I guess you had to take allergy medicine before you visited her, huh?"

"I always told her that I wasn't going to put medicine in my body, just so a cat's life could be more pleasant. Oh no, I'm an all-natural kind of girl. I don't even like to take vitamins."

"So what did you guys do?"

"If she wanted me to come visit, she had to change something about the cat. Like, keep him locked up. Thankfully, Ernest agreed with me. He was allergic, too."

I made a mental note of that fact. "Sage kept Mr. Mouser locked up when you visited?"

"Mr. Mouser was supposedly hypoallergenic. He

still made my allergies go crazy, though."

So Sage had purchased one of those hypoallergenic cats herself. Interesting.

Thyme shook her head. "Anyway, enough of that. I wanted to mention that the funeral is Saturday."

My hopes deflated at the conversation change. Still, I had learned a few new things. I forced a smile. "Thanks. People at the office have been asking."

She shook her head. "I still can't believe I'm having to plan my sister's funeral. I'm supposed to be in Aruba right now. So much for my dream vacation."

"I'm sorry. Were you and Sage close?"

She picked at a string on the couch cushion. "Close enough. I mean, we fought like cats and dogs when we were young. But we'd gotten close over the past few years. Hard times will do that to people."

"You mean, after she was accused of killing her husband?" I licked my lips, wondering if my approach had been the best one. But, for a moment, I had a feeling I looked more like a cat eyeing a canary for lunch than someone asking a casual question.

Her eyes widened. "You know about that?"

I nodded, hoping I hadn't just offended her. Or looked like a cat on the prowl, for that matter. "I do. It sounds like a difficult time."

"No one else stood beside her during that trial, so I did. Sisters are supposed to stick together, you know? Sisters look out for each other."

"Not even your mom or brother supported her during the trial?"

"They were there too. But most people thought she was guilty."

Ouch. "You thought she loved Ernest, despite their age difference?"

She nodded. "Yeah. It was weird. But I think he got her. She glowed when she was around him."

Someone had once told me that I glowed around Chad. Maybe unlikely pairs could work. Or maybe they'd literally end up just killing each other.

"Thyme, I heard Ernest left Sage a lot of money, but she donated all of it to charities."

Thyme nodded. "She did. That way there would be no hard feelings from his family and people would stop calling her a gold digger. She had to get a job again, start working and fend for herself."

"Still, that must have been a hard choice. I mean, Ernest had a lot of money."

"My sister didn't mind working. She even worked while they were married. But she was also clever. She did donate all of the money, but she set up her own nonprofit as a part of that."

I blinked, unsure if I'd heard her correctly. "Why would she do that?"

And why was Thyme being so forthcoming with the information?

"To ensure she still had money to use as she saw fit. She said there were a few things that needed some funding and that Ernest would understand."

Wow, Sage was a little devious. I wasn't sure if I was impressed or appalled. "Did she use it for her own personal gain?"

"Not really. I mean, look at her apartment. She wasn't living a rich lifestyle. No, she saw herself more as a crusader, and she had some projects she was working on. She named me as the President for this nonprofit, and then used the funds to accomplish what she needed to accomplish."

"And what was that? What was she trying to

accomplish?"

Thyme shrugged again. "I'm not sure. She never really said. What she said, exactly, was that it was a better idea if I didn't know."

"No hints even?"

"Only that no one was going to rake her husband's name through the mud and make him look foolish."

What if this somehow tied in with Paws and Fur Balls? What if Ernest had donated money to the organization, but Bryan had somehow mishandled the funds? Bryan was the one, after all, who made most of the financial decisions for the company. He'd said I could look at the books, but he could be trying to throw me off of his trail. I wondered, for that matter, if the nonprofit I worked for had ever utilized the lab where Andre worked? Somehow, this all tied in together.

Another theory started to surface in my mind. What if Tom found out about this nonprofit that Sage set up? What if he wanted to get the ultimate revenge on his stepmom? Money could truly make people do horrible things.

"Thyme, did any of Ernest's children ever find out about the nonprofit?"

She shrugged. "Not that I know of. They'd be burning mad if they did."

"What about his youngest son? Do you know him?"

"Tom? Sure I do. He was the nastiest one out of them all. He loves money, and don't let him tell you any different. It wouldn't surprise me if he was the one who poisoned Ernest."

"You think he would kill his own dad?"

"For money? Sure I do. The man lives for money. He'd sell his soul to be rich."

I nodded, more motives and theories solidifying in

my head. "Thanks for your time."

***

Just as I left, my cell phone rang. It was Chad. I wanted to avoid talking to him. I hated the way my heart thudded with sadness when I thought about our time apart. I hadn't realized just how much I cared about him until I wasn't with him anymore. But I didn't want him to track me down again.

"Hello?" I answered.

"Sierra?" Chad sounded confused. Who had he expected to answer? A police officer who would inform him I'd died?

"Yes?"

"You don't sound like yourself."

"I'm just irritated." I unlocked my car, but checked the backseat before getting inside. It was clear.

"Sorry to hear that. You're staying safe, right?"

Maybe he did care. "I'm trying to."

"Not to sound like a broken record, but any updates on someone to take the cats? My landlord just stopped by again. I really think the farther you are away from your cats right now, the safer all of you will be."

"I'm working on it." I really needed to move that up on my priority list. "I'm really sorry, Chad."

I miss you. I love you. I wish I could hit a rewind button. I didn't say the words, though. Why was I so stubborn?

"I thought you might say that, so I had an idea. I'm going to take the cats to Pastor Randy's house. He offered to keep them there and said that cats don't bother him."

"But—" I locked my doors before cranking my engine.

"I don't have any other choice. My landlord gave me an ultimatum. You know where Pastor Randy lives, right?"

My soul felt numb. "Yes, I do."

"Perfect." He paused, and an eternity seemed to pass in that moment. "Do you have any time to talk tonight, Sierra?"

I almost said yes. But then I remembered Freckles. I remembered how my time was ticking away. I'd have to talk to Chad after I got my cat back. I had no other choice.

"I'm kind of busy tonight. Maybe on Saturday?" Meg's words came back to me. *If someone didn't love my cats, I'd know they weren't the love of my life.* My heart lurched at the thought.

"Really? You can't even spare a few minutes?" His voice sounded calm but confused.

My heart squeezed. "Unfortunately, no."

"Is this because you're searching for your cat still?"

"You know how much they mean to me."

His silence said enough. It set me on edge. Made me feel judged and inadequate.

"Chad, why are you acting like this?" I finally asked.

"Why am I acting like this? Me? I've been bending over backwards to appease you."

Fire rushed through my blood. "Appease me? You just want me to do things your way."

"You mean because I want you to go to the police? That's only because I care about you, Sierra. Why can't you see that?"

"If you cared about me, you'd stop trying to get me to choose between my cats and the police. You would try harder to understand the position I'm in!"

"I've been biting my tongue. I've been trying to be nice even though I've only felt hostility from you. I don't think you would have given me the time of day this week if I hadn't been taking care of your cats. I feel like you're taking advantage of me."

I hit my hand against the steering wheel. "*I'm* taking advantage of *you*? All you've done is insult my cats and made me feel like I'm an inconvenience to you."

"Insult them? Are you crazy? I've gone out of my way to take care of them and try to make you happy. I wish the sentiment was reciprocated."

He'd gone out of his way? He was the crazy one. He'd just thrown me a bone and tried to pacify me.

"All I've heard is you complaining about how I'm not who you want me to be. You want to change me! Even worse—you want to control me!" I sucked in a deep breath before blurting, "You're just like my father!"

I didn't know where the words came from. From some place deep and painful, apparently. I hadn't truly realized how much of the way I was acting stemmed from my childhood. From hurt places in me. From my desire to rebel against people's expectations.

Silence stretched between us. I was breathing deeply, my heart pounding rapidly, and my thoughts racing.

"Sierra—" Chad started.

"I've got to go," I blurted.

I hit the END button. I had to stop doing that. Every time I turned around, I was hastily ending my phone calls with Chad in an effort to avoid talking about things I didn't want to talk about.

As I stared at my phone, I felt worse than ever. What was wrong with me? I had the ability to make things right, but I didn't. I didn't want to have to choose between my furry friends and the man of my dreams. Besides that, he wasn't even asking me to. Not really, at least.

That made me dumb.

Despite the fact I'd graduated from Yale.

That I'd won awards.

That my IQ was about 20 points higher than the average person's.

And what was all of that about Chad being like my dad? I squeezed back tears. Maybe it had to do with the fact that the man who'd played the biggest role in my upbringing had never accepted me for who I was. He'd wanted me to be the person he'd dreamed for me.

A doctor, just like him. To marry a good Japanese man. To live a quiet life.

Instead, I was a noisy, single animal rights activist.

My dad and I almost never spoke anymore except sometimes on holidays.

Though I was proud of my accomplishments and who I'd become, the fact always lingered in the back of my mind that the one person who should love me unconditionally, didn't love me at all. He'd practically shunned me and, in return, I'd shunned him, as well.

I pushed aside those thoughts. I didn't need a man in my life. Not my dad. Not Chad. Not anyone.

Right now, I had to think of my cats. Here I hadn't wanted to investigate. I'd wanted to let the police handle this.

But then someone had to pull my cats into this.

***

Where now? I could stop by Paws and Fur Balls. But perhaps my energy would be best spent at the moment if I looked out for the rights—and lives—of my own animals. After all, that's what I did for a career. I was an animal rights activist. Sometimes, you had to take care of your own. I would *not* be my parents.

With that in mind, I swung by Harbor Park—the stadium where our minor league baseball team the Tides played—and bought a ticket. I had suspicions that Tom was hiding something and that his vacation here in Virginia Beach was no accident. He'd claimed he got here Saturday evening, but why should I believe him?

My theory was that he'd found out about the nonprofit Sage had set up. What she'd done was slimy; even I had to admit that. And it just might have been enough to put Tom over the edge. She came across looking like a saint, all the while she still had access to some of her former husband's money.

Amidst the smell of hot dogs, popcorn, and an organ playing "Take Me Out to the Ballgame," I searched for Tom. I spotted him behind first base, sitting with a plump brunette and a gangly preteen holding a baseball mitt. A free seat beside Tom seemed to call my name, so I plopped down there, as if I belonged.

He did a double take when he saw me.

"Hello, Tom," I muttered.

Sweat instantly appeared on his forehead. "You? What are *you* doing here?"

"I have a few more questions."

He looked over his shoulder. "Did you follow me?"

"No, I saw the tickets in your hands when I met with you earlier this week."

His wife—a regal, almost mean looking woman with coifed brown hair—peered over at me and scowled. "Did you bring a friend, Tom?"

"Long story," he muttered. "How about we take a quick walk?"

I smiled brightly. "It sounds like a plan."

We climbed the steps to the upper deck and

wandered between the crowds. I could feel the nervous energy radiating off of Tom as we walked. "Why are you here, Sierra?"

"Tom, I know that Sage—or maybe I should call her Anise—set up a supposed nonprofit and then donated a large portion of your father's money to that organization."

He scowled ever so slightly before catching himself and neutralizing his expression. "That's the first I've ever heard of such."

"I don't think that's true. In fact, I think that's why you planned your vacation here, to the very area where she moved. I think you wanted to confront her about it."

"That's crazy. Why would I do that? What good would it do for me to confront her? The money is rightfully hers." He tugged at the bill of his baseball cap. The hat covered his receding hairline and made him look about ten years younger.

I shrugged. "If it makes you feel any better, she wasn't living extravagantly. In fact, I'm pretty sure she was living off of the money she made at Paws and Fur Balls. I'm not sure what she was using that other money for."

He stared at me.

"Did you come here just to kill her and get your final revenge?" Maybe I should learn to be more subtle? On second thought, there was a time to be subtle and a time to be direct. Now wasn't the time to hold back.

That accusation seemed to jostle him to life. "Are you out of your mind? I would never kill someone!"

"But you did know that she'd funneled that money into another account?"

He stared at me again before slowly nodding. "Yes, I did know about that. I wasn't happy. But I didn't kill her. I just wanted to talk to her."

"And tell her what a lousy human being she was? I

read some of the articles on the court case. I think you were the most upset of all your siblings." The articles hadn't said that, but I didn't want to throw Thyme under the bus, so to speak.

"Yeah, I was upset." His face reddened as he crossed his arms. "I don't deny that."

"So that whole story about your friend who'd won the lottery? You made that up?" We stopped in front of a gift shop to finish our conversation.

"No, I actually did have a friend who won the lottery. He did end up with a miserable life. But here's the whole truth. My *stepmom*," he said the word with disdain, "didn't deserve that money. My brother and sisters and I did. Anise—Sage, as you guys call her—swept into my dad's life for a couple of years and ended up with his entire fortune. She had my dad wrapped around her little finger."

I moved to the side as a family of six squeezed past. "It sounds to me like it's your dad you should be mad at. Why in the world didn't he have you in his will?"

His scowl deepened. "He thought *we* only loved him for his money, and we thought *Anise* only loved him for his money."

"A tangled web, indeed." Families were complicated. That was for sure.

"You can say that again. In the end, Anise won."

"Sounds like motive for murder to me."

He clenched his jaw before responding. "I have an alibi. I didn't get into town until Saturday evening. I gave in and listened to the local news after we talked so I could hear more about her death. The report said she died Friday afternoon."

"You did your research since we last talked."

His face continued to redden. "You know who you

need to look into? Her sister. Thyme."

"Why would I look into Thyme?"

"Because Thyme is the one who told me about the supposed nonprofit. She sold her sister out."

"Why would she do that?"

"Apparently, she thought she was going to get part of the cut if she helped her sister. She didn't. Maybe she thought if her sister ended up dead, she would finally get some of the money she was due."

"How do you know that?"

His scowl was replaced by a smug, satisfied grin. "Thyme told me. In fact, she was supposed to be in Aruba now, right after she blackmailed her sister for some money."

CHAPTER 15

"Why would Thyme tell you that?"

Tom paused and put his hands on his hips. "She wanted more money. She'd stood by her sister during the entire trial. She thought her loyalty deserved a reward."

"Did Sage know that her sister had sold her out?"

He nodded. "She found out and she was furious. Sage immediately removed her as president of her fake nonprofit. Last I heard, they hadn't spoken in several months."

"But Thyme is here now to help plan the funeral. And that just so happens to be the same week you're in town."

He sighed. "Okay, look. It's like this. No, it wasn't a coincidence that I came to Virginia Beach on vacation. I did want to talk to Sage. Thyme had tried to blackmail her, but it hadn't worked. I was going to try my hand at it."

"And when she wouldn't give you the money, you killed her?"

He wiped the sweat from his brow and glanced around, as if to make sure no one had heard me. "No. I would never kill her. I'd just want to drag her name through the mud with the media and exposé her for who she really is."

"What about Thyme? Would she murder for money?" I remembered the red, tear-filled eyes she'd had the first time I saw her. I'd assumed she was weeping over her sister. Had it really just been allergies?

"It's like this. Sage was worth more alive than she was dead. Now that she's gone, none of us have anything. She left everything she had to Paws and Fur Balls. Her net worth wasn't much, but Thyme didn't get a cent."

"Tom, when exactly did you get into town again?"

"Saturday evening." He scowled. "Want me to prove it?"

"Can you?"

"Of course." He pulled out his cell phone and typed something in. The next moment, he showed me an electronic ticket on the screen. "There's my flight in. I couldn't have killed Sage. I was in Oregon."

***

Back at my apartment, I tried to process everything.

I rubbed my temples, wishing life as it was at this moment would simply disappear. But, since it wouldn't, I decided to make a few phone calls and try to find someone to keep an eye on my cats for me. Everyone seemed to have an excuse.

If I wanted to maintain any kind of self-respect, I was going to have to take my cats from Chad and bring them back to my place. I'd stay with them all day, if that's what I had to do to protect them. The problem was, if I stayed here all day to keep an eye on them, then I couldn't hit the streets to track down whoever was doing this.

Therefore, I was in a quandary.

I set aside those thoughts for a moment, and, out of curiosity, looked up Brandon Channel, the guy who'd come up with these hypoallergenic cats. I wasn't buying the whole concept, but I needed to do some research before I formed too many judgments.

The company was called BioCare, and it was founded by Brandon Channel. Brandon, apparently, had a degree in biology and had spent five years researching what it was about cats that triggered allergic reactions in so many people. He claimed his was the first cat that was scientifically proven as hypoallergenic.

I scanned the rest of the information. The company claimed that a protein found in cats' saliva and skin called Fel d1 caused allergies. Brandon bred cats with lower instances of Fel d1, and the result was a feline that didn't trigger allergies in the same way.

There were yearlong wait lists. Price tags in the five digits. Moving testimonials.

However, there were no photos of Brandon, which surprised me.

There was an endorsement by Andre and his lab.

Now that was interesting. Andre had endorsed Brandon's cat? Maybe Andre was Brandon. Maybe he knew how to work the system, to make the lab results look believable.

Out of curiosity, I searched for complaints about BioCare. And, boy, did I find them. Apparently, Brandon Channel made everyone sign an ironclad contract that basically made it impossible to get any money back, even if the cat still made the new owners sneeze.

Impulsively, I went back to the company's website, grabbed their email address, and composed an email to them. I used a generic account I had, just so my name wouldn't be known. I had to be subtle here, because whoever wanted information from me obviously knew my name and what I looked like.

I wrote that I was very allergic to cats and interested in purchasing a cat from them. I'd done my research on their company and felt like we'd be a good fit.

I also explained that I'd loved cats, had always dreamed about having one, and when I heard about their company, I felt the first touch of hope that I had in years. Blah, blah, blah. I made sure to include that money was no issue. I even added that I'd received a nice life insurance payment from my late husband that would pay for the cat. For the final kick, I signed my name as Ivy Livingston.

It seemed like the name of someone who was older, someone a man like Brandon might want to take advantage of. I thought the money was important to mention and might encourage him to respond sooner.

I hit send. I doubted I'd hear anything, especially considering the waiting list, but it was worth a shot.

The information still fluttered around in my mind, though.

A secret nonprofit used to funnel a dead spouse's funds.

A man pretending to have developed a miracle cat.

A research lab testing allergens.

A faceless CEO of a company raking in big money.

What did you get when you put all of that together? Could Brandon Channel be more than one person? A team of people in cahoots with one another?

For that matter, maybe Tom and Thyme were both working together? Maybe they were plotting to somehow get their own share of money they felt entitled to?

Or maybe Bryan had mishandled some funds donated by Ernest, and Sage had come here to pay revenge.

Rupert . . . his only connection was Chicago, unless there was something I was missing. Murdering one of his own employees didn't seem like something a successful businessman would do. Unless he was certain he wouldn't be caught. However, he'd just come to town on Sunday night. He wasn't even here when Sage died, so I could probably rule him out.

There was still the fact that someone—most likely Bryan—had a crush on Sage. Unrequited love had started wars. Certainly it could be cause for murder.

What *was* I missing?

I had to figure it out if I wanted to get back to my regularly scheduled life. And, boy, did I ever want to do that.

CHAPTER 16

An hour later, my cell phone rang. I didn't recognize the number—it was an out-of-state area code—but I answered anyway.

"This is Sierra."

"Sierra, it's Rupert."

I straightened. "Hi there. How are you?"

"It's almost the end of the week. I wondered if you had an answer for me yet? Will you be taking over Paws and Fur Balls?"

I nibbled on my bottom lip a moment. "I still haven't decided, Rupert. I'm afraid this week has been a bit hectic."

"I see. I'm coming back into town on Monday. I was hoping to start the process by then. I really think you're the person to do this job, Sierra."

"I'm so flattered. Can you give me until tomorrow?"

"Until tomorrow. But I'm afraid that's all the time I can give."

"I appreciate that, sir. Thank you."

I hung up, still trying to process all of my thoughts. They were just giving me a headache. I didn't want to be in the middle of all of this. But, even more than that, I wanted my cats to be safe.

So I resisted my urge to abandon this investigation. I resisted the impulse to pull the covers over my head and ignore this mystery. I was Sierra Nakamura. I was a fighter.

With that thought, I hopped on my computer to do

some more research and saw that I had an email from BioCare. I blinked in surprise at their quick response. By some miracle, the company had a cat that seemed to fit the description of what I wanted. In fact, if I sent them a one thousand dollar deposit, they'd hold the cat for me. They even sent a picture of a beautiful black feline with striking green eyes and told me they just happened to have a representative in town.

What happened to the yearlong wait lists? Was that a fabrication to make the cats seem more popular and therefore more valuable?

If these cats weren't hypoallergenic, then where exactly was this company getting their felines from? Were they breeding cats in their home and trying to pass them off as "special"? If not in their homes, then where?

Out of curiosity, I jumped onto a local online website that advertised pets for sale. I searched for kittens that were eight-weeks-old and black. I scrolled through tons of pictures.

Finally, I found the exact same picture that BioCare had sent me. It had been cut and pasted from online. This woman was selling her litter of kittens for only $50 each, however. BioCare was charging $25,000.

Outrage blazed through me.

I jotted down the number listed on the online ad and grabbed my phone. A woman answered on the second ring.

"I'm calling about a cat you advertised online. An all black cat with striking green eyes. Please tell me he's still available."

"Wouldn't you know a woman just bought him about ten minutes ago?"

A *woman*? What? I hadn't been expecting that.

"Oh, no. I missed Black Beauty. That's what I was going to

name him. That's too bad. I'm hoping my daughter bought him for me. Please tell me the woman who came by was skinny with dark hair. Please! I'll be heartbroken if you don't."

The woman laughed. "I don't want to give away any surprises."

"Come on now. You're ruining my birthday."

"Well, I can't ruin a birthday," she murmured. "Here's what I can say. You could very well have a cat waiting for you."

I squealed. "Thank you, thank you, thank you."

"Don't thank me yet," she said with a laugh. "But happy birthday."

I hung up and only one face stood out in my mind now. Thyme. She had to be the one behind this.

I turned back to my computer, ready to type out a response to my email. "Is there any way I can see the cat before I send the deposit? I've heard about too many online scams. I get very nervous about these things."

I hit SEND and stared at the computer screen, wondering how the company would respond to that. When would I hear back? In time to save Freckles?

I pushed out images of someone hurting my precious cat. How could someone be this cruel? It was almost like the person behind these threats knew exactly how to get to me.

But Thyme wouldn't know that. Nor would Tom. And BioCare just happened to have a representative in town. Both Thyme and Tom were in town. Maybe they were working together.

The answers seemed so close, yet so far away.

A reply came back immediately. "I can meet tomorrow with the cat."

My pulse raced. I nibbled on my lip as I typed my

response. "Name the time and place, and I'll be there."

Five minutes later, I had the name of a park and a time to meet.

Finally, I was getting somewhere.

Maybe, just maybe, I could relieve my state of anxiety. My state of feeling like a cat on a hot tin roof.

And maybe, just maybe, I could finally get Freckles back.

***

As I scooted myself away from my desk, a picture fluttered to the floor. I bent down and picked it up.

It was a photo of Chad and me. At the beach. His arm was around my shoulders and I had a dopey grin across my face.

Love could do that to you.

Had I just said love?

That's what we had. I loved Chad. I'd known that for a long time.

I'd been an idiot this week.

I'd overreacted this week. And, for some deep psychological reason, I was projecting my feelings toward my father onto Chad. I was ruining one of the best relationships in my life, and I had no idea what to do about it.

Spontaneously, I grabbed my car keys and hurried out to my car. I headed to Pastor Randy's place, almost surprising myself that I was going there instead of to Chad's. But I needed someone to talk to, and Pastor Randy knew Chad.

I'd been to his place before. Gabby had brought me to a Bible study and I'd liked it okay enough. I just didn't think the whole religion thing was for me.

I pounded on the door to Pastor Randy's small but neat house. A moment later, he pulled the door open. When he spotted me, he smiled. "Sierra! Come to check on your cats?"

"Yes. Kind of." I shifted on the porch, suddenly anxious. "I think I need to have a time of confession. You don't have some kind of booth at your church, do you?"

A wrinkle formed between his eyes. "Booth? No, not quite."

"Do you practice confession?"

"Not as much as we should. But confessing our wrongs is healthy. I encourage people to do it more." He nodded affably.

I swallowed hard, nerves getting the best of me. "I need to confess something, then."

He opened the door farther and swept his hand toward the living room. "Why don't you come inside? We can talk, and you can love on your cats some."

I nodded and stepped inside. It was kind of weird to be with Pastor Randy alone. It was kind of weird to be seeking counsel from a minister, period. Some might say that God worked everything for a higher purpose and that He'd worked it out so that the pastor would have my cats and I would be here.

I wasn't sure I believed any of that, though the idea did sometimes have its appeal. I'd never thought my friend Gabby—a huge skeptic—would ever change her way of thinking. But I guess a few near brushes with death had opened her eyes.

I sat on his couch and picked up Mr. Mouser. Poor cat. He'd been through so much.

"What's on your mind, Sierra?" Shaggy pulled up a dining room chair and sat across from me.

It wasn't exactly a confessional booth, nor was I

anonymous. But this would have to work. "Never once in my entire life have I questioned my priorities and my ways of doing things. Until now."

"What happened to cause this change?"

I shook my head, not believing the words I wanted to say would actually come from my mouth. "Chad happened. I've been miserable this week because we've been fighting. I've realized how much I do care about him."

"That's a good thing."

"Except, I think I may have pushed him over the edge. I was being stubborn and standing my ground about not getting the police involved in something I was investigating because it would put my cats in danger. And I do love my cats. But I love Chad, too." Despite how I'd royally screwed things up between us lately.

"Have you told him that?"

I shook my head and pulled Mr. Mouser closer to me. "Not yet. My pride keeps getting in the way. I keep hoping he'll meet me halfway or he'll initiate a conversation." Was that what he'd been trying to do earlier? I couldn't be sure. I was so blinded by my own feelings and agenda.

Pastor Randy leaned forward, looking all . . . well, pastor like. "Maybe you're both being stubborn. Or maybe somewhere along the line your communication has broken down."

"Check and check, on both counts." I rubbed my hands against my jeans. "The problem is that I don't know how to make things right."

"Maybe you should have this conversation with Chad instead of me."

"I know! But something's holding me back."

"What's that?"

"I know things will have to change. On one hand, I want that change. I want compromise. On the other hand, I fear it."

"Love can require sacrifice—on both ends."

I watched him, waiting for what I was sure would come next. It didn't. "Aren't you going to tell me about Jesus now and how He practiced the ultimate sacrifice when He died on the cross to give us life?"

"It sounds like you already know."

"Gabby's mentioned it a few times. I've studied the Bible, you know. It's a fascinating text."

"It can be more than that."

"Agnosticism is in my blood."

"It doesn't have to be." He leaned forward. "Look, there are a lot of things I value about the Christian life. For the sake of this conversation, I'll keep it simple. Before I had Christ in my life, I lived for myself. I lived for today, for the temporary. When I became a Christian, I was able to live for a greater good. A greater good than even saving all of the animals on the earth. I found hope beyond the failures I see in this world today."

All of the deep thoughts in the world did nothing for me at the moment, and that realization made me uncomfortable enough that I fell back on my typical spiel. My animal talk spiel. "Do you think Jesus would be a vegan?"

He stared at me and shook his head as if my question had startled him. "What?"

I raised a hand, wishing I hadn't gone there. "Never mind."

"Wait, I think I can speak on this for a moment."

"Really?" I had no hope that he actually had an answer for me.

He nodded. "Sure. In the book of Matthew, it says

that not a single sparrow will fall to the ground outside of our Father's care. In Luke, it says not one of them is forgotten by God. I'd say that God cares an awful lot about His creations, even the feathered ones."

I chewed on his words for a moment. "Those are comforting Scriptures," I conceded.

"In fact, the Bible often compares Jesus to a shepherd who'd give His life for His sheep."

"The Good Shepherd. That's definitely admirable." I squeezed my lips together a moment. I knew how people usually reacted when I asked questions like this. But I really wanted to know, even if it made me sound like a seven-year-old. "Do you think animals go to heaven?"

After all, how could God be loving if animals didn't reunite with their owners in heaven?

He cringed before relaxing his shoulders again. "I can't say for sure. But I do know that in Revelation 6, it's mentioned that there are horses in heaven. In fact, later on in Revelation 19, it says there will be enough horses for a vast army to ride."

"Really?" Hope pricked inside me. Maybe God was a loving God. Maybe He was at least worth considering.

He nodded. "God didn't even permit the eating of meat back in the Garden of Eden—not even for the animals. Instead, He gave them every green plant for food. It wasn't until Noah that he granted people that permission."

"I never realized that." I shook my head, trying to let everything sink in. "Look, I get what you're saying—about everything from animals to the way life should be lived. I feel like I do live my life for a greater purpose than myself. I live it to save animals. That's why it's so weird that I'm thinking about putting a person over my life's mission."

"It doesn't have to be one or the other. I'm sure Jesus loves it that you love His creations so much."

I hated to admit it, but the pastor seemed pretty wise.

The ideals that the pastor presented did have their appeal. But I wasn't about to drop to my knees and convert. No, I was the thought out type who took my time making big life decisions.

At least, I had been. Maybe I needed to mix things up more.

I had noticed that Gabby seemed awfully content since she'd changed her life. At times, I thought that would be nice. I thought it would be nice to not put so much of my hopes—and on the other end of the spectrum, my worries—in the things happening in this life.

At once, I wondered what my parents would think if they knew I was even considering embracing religion. They were intellectuals, business-minded, success-oriented, and non-emotive. I wondered what it would be like to have a Heavenly Father who loved me just as I was. I still couldn't get the image of my own father out of my mind, though.

Demanding. Exacting. Disapproving.

I stood, not sure what exactly my "confessional" had accomplished. At least I'd gotten a few things off my chest. "I guess I can take my cats back."

"They can stay here, if you want."

I blinked in surprise. Had I heard him correctly? "Really?"

"Of course. If that will help you out." He offered an easy grin.

Now, why couldn't Chad say stuff like that? And why did I put these expectations on him? I should accept him, just like I wanted to be accepted.

The pastor shifted again. "Look, Sierra. I don't want to step into something where I'm not welcome. I can say this, though. Chad wants to help you. He felt terrible when he had to bring your cats here, and he made me promise to look out for them. He said the cats were important to you."

My heart welled with appreciation. "I appreciate your time, Pastor."

"Any time you want to talk, Sierra. Any time."

It was then that an idea hit. A pretty brilliant idea, if I did say so myself. But it would take some planning. "Pastor Randy, I do have one more favor, if you're up for it."

He raised an eyebrow. "What are you thinking?"

I sat down and explained my idea to him.

Then I realized my cats couldn't stay here. At least, not tonight. Thankfully, I had a plan for where I could take them for the evening. I only hoped my gut instinct was right.

CHAPTER 17

The next morning, I was all set to meet with this Brandon guy. I'd written up a spiel, and I was meeting with Pastor Shaggy early so we could go over it.

The pastor hadn't been one hundred percent behind this. Not even fifty percent behind it, truth be told. He'd said I should let the authorities handle it. He'd also said he had a problem with using a cover story. Something about it being untruthful.

I'd promised him I'd think of a way to make it work and keep it honest.

Then I'd gotten home and thought about ways to make it honest, but come up with nothing.

That meant that my meeting this morning would be interesting, to say the least.

I was supposed to meet Brandon at an area called Waterside. It was a shopping and dining area located on the Elizabeth River in downtown Norfolk. A seawall with benches overlooking boats and a passenger ferry and an old battleship-turned-museum stretched beside the water there.

First, I was going to meet the pastor inside the food court area so we could go over everything. I arrived early and tried not to pace as I waited.

But the pieces were starting to come together and form a clear picture in my mind now.

I'd done an Internet search last night and discovered that Sage's late husband had been one of the initial investors in BioCare. Thyme had said Ernest was allergic to cats, so I pictured him investing in the company in an effort to make the love of his life happy and to be able to get a cat. When they got the cat, they realized the whole thing was a scam. They went to confront Brandon, but he'd disappeared.

When Ernest died and the trial was finally over, Sage put all of her energy into tracking Brandon down. Maybe that's why she'd set up that nonprofit of her own. She wanted to burn the man who'd taken advantage of her husband. Besides, Sage had said Ernest sustained stress in the days before he died. Could it have been over a bad investment in BioCare? I thought it was a good theory.

My guess was that Brandon knew she was on to him and didn't want his company to be destroyed. When he had the right opportunity, he'd killed her.

I still wasn't sure about what "information" exactly he was looking for. I figured it was the dirt Sage had collected on him, but I didn't know where that was. I'd have to cross that bridge later.

I was fairly certain that Brandon Channel wasn't his real name. I could only find mentions of him in the past four years, and there were never any pictures. That was a red flag right there. Most entrepreneurs were more than willing to plaster their pictures everywhere possible.

Now, if I could just nail down who exactly Brandon Channel was, I could turn his name over to the police. I would have done my duty.

Better yet, my cats would be safe.

I was putting my bets on Thyme as the culprit, though. She made the most sense. But I also wondered if she was working with someone. She almost had to be. After all, a *man* had threatened me in my car. I was certain of it.

As I waited, I opened my purse and saw some

remaining glass shards there. I took out my wallet, jammed it under my arm, and stuffed the shock collar—still in my purse from that meeting earlier this week—into one jean pocket and my lip balm and keys into the other. Then I shook my purse out over a trashcan.

I'd just put my wallet back in when I heard someone approaching. I squinted at the face I saw. It wasn't Pastor Randy. It was . . .

"Chad?" Not only was he here, but he was wearing a suit and a tie, and he'd shaved and combed his hair. "What are you doing here?"

"Randy sent me." Chad frowned.

"Why would he do that?" I stuffed my keys back into my purse and pulled it onto my shoulder.

"He said he couldn't sleep last night and wasn't comfortable doing this. Yet, he also said if he didn't come, you'd come alone and then possibly die."

"He told you what I was doing?" Outrage burst through me like a tiger bounding after its prey. "Isn't that a breach of something? Don't pastors have to keep your secrets?"

"Maybe you're thinking of priests? I don't know. But my apartment was broken into yesterday."

My heart sped until it was a dull thud in my ears. "What? Why?"

"Your guess is as good as mine. But, probably for your cats. I figured Randy was right and you shouldn't be here alone. So here I am." He slapped his hands against his hips, as if he had no choice in coming.

"You're going to help me?" I clarified.

"That's right. Do you have a problem with that?"

"No. It's just that we don't have a lot of time. I've got to brief you." I straightened his collar. "You dressed up. That's good. You clean up nicely."

"I'm uncomfortable with this, on more than one level."

I remembered my conversation with the pastor and my revelations about myself. I had to make things right with Chad. I had to own up to my own weaknesses, something I'd never been good at doing. But, for the sake of our relationship, it had to be done.

However, this wasn't the time or place.

"I appreciate you," I started.

And I'm sorry. The words wouldn't dislodge themselves from my throat. Later, I told myself.

I licked my lips instead. "Whoever's behind this obviously recognizes me. I can't take the chance. They'll run as soon as they spot me."

"So, what am I supposed to tell this guy?" He smoothed his tie.

"That you're the grandson of Ivy Livingston. She's not feeling well and can't make it, but she desperately wants this cat."

"And when he asks where the $25,000 is?"

"First, you read the contract. You need to have issues with it. Serious issues."

"Okay."

"Then say that in good conscience you can't sign it, not when you consider the amount of money you have to pay. You need a money back guarantee."

"I can handle that much."

"And whatever you do, don't look over here. I don't want to draw attention to myself. Understand?"

"Of course."

I patted him on the back, only it turned out to be more like a shove. "Knock 'em dead."

"Great choice of words."

I turned his phone on, dialed my number, and slid it

into his pocket. "A trick I learned from Gabby." I hit MUTE on my own phone so nothing would be amplified, coming from his pocket. "This way I can hear everything that's being said."

I pulled my hat down low and found a seat behind a huge potted plant, so I could still keep my eye on Chad. He, in the meantime, found a seat on a bench.

Now, I just had to wait.

Chad looked uncomfortable—probably more because of the suit than the situation.

My heart lurched as I watched him. I loved him, I realized again. I didn't think I'd ever believe those words. But, if our time apart had proven anything, it was that I felt strongly for him.

I needed to stop being so prideful and let him know.

Except, I couldn't do that now.

Chad couldn't hear me, but I could hear him. He was mumbling something under his breath, and he looked back at me.

I offered him a smile.

Which must have confused him, because he scrunched his eyebrows together. "We've got to talk sometime, Sierra," he muttered. I understood him this time.

I couldn't read him, though. Talk about making this break up final? Probably. I'd most likely pushed him too far. I'd ruined the best relationship to ever happen to me.

Before I could think about it anymore, I saw someone familiar in the distance.

Andre? What was he doing here? Was he behind this?

He walked toward Chad's bench. I bristled, waiting to see what he'd do. He got closer and closer.

But he kept going.

My gaze swerved to the far side of the shopping area. His lab was around here somewhere, wasn't it? What were the chances he was here for his lunch break?

I wasn't sure, but I was on edge.

The last thing I wanted was to pull Chad into a dangerous situation. I'd already ruined his couch and nearly had him kicked out of his apartment.

But when I looked up, Andre had spotted me. He was headed my way.

I had to make a choice: Fight or flight.

CHAPTER 18

"Are you following me?" Andre demanded.

I could see the veins at his neck bulging.

This wasn't good.

I made sure I remained hidden behind the tree. Despite however scary Andre appeared right now, I would not blow this whole operation. "No. Why would you ask that?"

"You just so happen to be here today?" His nostrils flared.

"I'm actually waiting for someone else." I decided to turn the tables on him. "Maybe the question should be: What are you doing here?"

"I walk here every day on my lunch break."

"A likely excuse."

His jaw dropped. "What are you implying?"

"I'm implying that I'm investigating the murder of Anise Wentworth, and you're on my list."

He glared down at me. "I was on Anise's side. I was trying to help her nail the criminals who were ripping people off."

"And who would that be?"

He looked away for a minute, his jaw locking in place. I didn't think he was going to tell me. But then he turned back toward me. "I never got his real name. He went by Brandon Channel. He could be anyone."

"Why'd you want to help her?" I looked back at Chad and saw that he was still alone and waiting. Good. I didn't want to miss anything.

"Because this Brandon Channel took the findings I produced for him on this hypoallergenic cat, and he twisted my words. He made it sound like I endorsed his company. Do you know what that does to my professional reputation? I'm the laughing stock among my colleagues. Everyone knows there's no such thing as a hypoallergenic cat."

"I agree."

"I contacted him and asked him to remove my endorsement from his site. He didn't respond. I hired a lawyer. My lawyer couldn't track him down. So my endorsement remains on this man's website."

"How did Sage—I mean, Anise—play into all of this?"

"She thought this man was scamming people and she wanted to bust him."

"Did she say why?"

"She only hinted at it. My impression is that this man had scammed her husband out of a good deal of money. There may have been more to the story than that. I mean, from what I understand, her husband was loaded. Yes, it's a shame that he lost a five million dollar investment. But was it reason enough that she should make it her life's work to nail this guy?" He shrugged. "I couldn't tell you."

Another theory began to swirl in my mind. I wondered if it could be correct. I needed more time to chew on it.

I glanced at Chad again. He was still alone.

Andre leaned toward me. "If you do find this guy, give me a minute alone with him. Please."

***

Brandon Channel was fifteen minutes late. Chad was getting antsy. I was getting antsy.

But we still waited. This was my only chance at catching this guy and saving Freckles. I had to use every ounce of my patience.

Finally, I saw someone else approaching Chad with a cat carrier in hand.

But it wasn't a man. It was . . . Kyla?

I hadn't seen this one coming.

"Excuse me, are you with BioCare?" Chad asked. He stood and eyed the cat carrier.

Kyla paused. "I am. But you don't fit the description of who I'm looking for."

"Ivy Livingston?"

"That's right."

"I'm her grandson. She wasn't feeling great this morning and asked me to come in her place."

Chad sounded very convincing. I was impressed.

I quickly thought back. Had Kyla and Chad met? I didn't think so. Chad had only been to my work once or twice to pick me up for lunch. I didn't think they'd ever seen each other.

Despite that, panic began to rise in me.

"And you are?" Chad asked.

"My name is Kyla." She extended her hand. She'd used her real name. Surprising.

"I was expecting a man."

"Is that right? Well, I'm hoping you were expecting a great new companion." She raised the carrier. "Because I've got just the cat for you."

"Oh, what a cute little kitty." I knew Chad well enough to hear the false excitement in his voice. He did like animals but he wasn't the gushing type. From the distance, I could see him stick his finger inside the carrier.

He was trying to look interested. I had to give him credit for that. "I think he'll be perfect for Grandma Ivy. She's a total cat freak, but she hasn't been able to have one as a pet."

"I know. Isn't that terrible when allergies hold you back from something you love?"

"Yeah, I mean, Grandma Ivy has a cat calendar. Cat placemats. Stuffed animal cats. She even has a cat attitude, you know what I mean? Superior and lofty. I think if she had to choose between her family and cats, she'd choose her cats."

Oh. My. Goodness. Chad was talking about me! The nerve of him.

"I think our company and this little cat will be a great fit with your grandmother then," Kyla continued.

"The thing about my grandma is that I'll always love her, even if she is crazy about her furry friends. Even if she thinks she understands me but doesn't. Grandma Ivy is also intelligent and loyal and cuddly. Kind of like cats."

My heart softened. He was talking to me now, I realized. Trying to tell me that he did accept me, cats and all.

"Your grandmother is cuddly?" Kyla asked. She shook her head. "Never mind. I don't want to know."

"Weird, right? But, if I didn't love her, I would never be here. Isn't that what love is about? Putting aside our own desires in order to make your loved one happy?"

"I suppose," Kyla muttered.

I smiled, my heart lifting for the first time all week. Maybe Chad and I weren't on different pages after all. We both had to learn to compromise. Our relationship was worth it.

Chad straightened. "From what I've read, you've done some amazing things with these cats and made it possible for people who've never been able to have a cat as a pet—I mean, animal companion—before to have one."

I had to smile again. All of these weeks of conditioning and he was finally learning.

"Yes, there's been a lot of research that's gone into this. We've made a lot of customers very happy. After all, a house isn't a home without a cat."

Chad chuckled, though it sounded tight. "No, it's not, is it?"

"Any other questions I can answer for you?"

"Is this science foolproof? What if my grandma is still allergic?"

"She won't be. Our results are very effective."

"Is that right? So it's satisfaction guaranteed?"

"You know it."

He nodded slowly. "Alright then. What's next?"

Kyla pulled something from her bag. "All I need is for you to sign this contract. It just has the basic terms of our agreement. Then I need that certified check, and we'll be good to go. You can take home this little cuddle bug all for yourself."

He rubbed his hands together. "Sounds great."

My foot started to twitch nervously. This is where it could all fall apart. Maybe I should have called the police.

Instead, I pulled out my phone, pretended to be texting, all while secretly taking pictures of the exchange going on across the way.

Maybe I finally had enough information that I could put this in the hands of the authorities. Just as I pulled my phone down, I heard something click behind me.

Before I could turn, I felt the barrel of a gun press into me.

"Hello, Sierra. Fancy seeing you here."

CHAPTER 19

I started to turn but the gun pressed harder into me.

"Don't draw attention to yourself," someone hissed in my ear.

I'd know that voice anywhere. I'd replayed it a million times in my head as I'd thought about my future.

"Rupert," I muttered, turning slightly until his face came into view. "I should have known."

He raised his eyebrows and glared at me. I'd never realized how beady his gaze looked before today.

"I thought you might be on to me," he snarled. "That's why I agreed to this little soirée. I had to make sure it was you. Now, I've got to get rid of collateral damage."

I stared straight ahead, wondering if anyone around us could tell something was wrong. Apparently not because no one even looked my way. Now I had to buy time. "I guess you don't make enough money with all your other businesses?"

"I made a few bad investments myself, and I was going to lose everything. That's when I had the idea to make people think hypoallergenic cats were real. They'd pay anything to have a furry friend. Pets are such a big business."

"You knew all along these cats weren't the real deal."

"Part of this is the power of suggestion, Sierra.

They believe the cats won't make them sneeze, so they don't. It's really a beautiful thing. And it helped me pay my bills. To keep businesses like Paws and Fur Balls open."

"There were other ways," I growled.

"Easy for you to say. Anise wanted to shut me down completely. I couldn't let that happen."

I glanced over at Chad. He still talked to Kyla. Clueless. "You pulled Kyla into this?"

"She thinks she's doing an exposé right now. I called in a personal favor. Said I was interested in naming her Executive Director. She had no idea. Even picked up the cat yesterday." He smirked.

"How can you live with yourself?" He was a cold-hearted manipulator. He used people like puppies used newspaper while becoming housebroken. Why would someone as wealthy as Rupert run this kind of scam?

"Easy. Money makes everything better." He nudged me. "Start walking."

"Everything you ever fought for . . . it was a lie." I'd thought he was a role model when, in truth, he was as greedy as anyone else. Maybe even more so, for that matter.

"I've never hurt any animals."

"You hurt animals at the top of the food chain. You killed a human."

He continued to prod me forward, one arm wrapped around my back. Anyone else might think we were out on a lovers' stroll. Little would they know I had a gun to my side.

"If Sage and her husband had minded their own business, we wouldn't be here right now. They just had to keep pushing, threatening everything I'd built. All of my hard work. It was going to be gone, just like that. Along with my reputation."

I sucked in a deep breath. "You killed Ernest, too, didn't you? That's what this is all really about. It's more than scamming people. Ernest was going to sue you and completely destroy everything you'd worked hard to build. You were the one who killed him."

Why, oh why, hadn't I realized that earlier? This was about so much more than hypoallergenic cats.

"Sage had to get sneaky on me. She just had to get a job at one of my companies in an effort to collect dirt on me and bust me. But I was on to her. That's why I made sure she got the Hessel's Hairstreak assignment. I wanted to catch her alone and confront her."

"You mean kill her?"

"I always knew you were a smart one." He pushed the gun harder. "Now, keep walking before anyone notices what we're doing over here. We have some things to talk about."

"Like what?"

He frowned. "Mr. Mouser, of course."

So this *was* about more than threatening my cats to get to me. Mr. Mouser had been the target all along.

"Why do you want Mr. Mouser back so badly? There are plenty of other cats you've sold that will prove you're a fraud." I kept my head high as we walked farther and farther away from Chad. I didn't want to show my fear, even if it was torpedoing inside me.

Details began clicking in my mind. Freckles and Mr. Mouser looked an awful lot alike. I wondered if Rupert had taken Freckles thinking she was Mr. Mouser? This could turn out very, very badly.

"Maybe you're not as smart as I thought you were." He walked closer. "Keep walking."

We slipped away from Chad. Had he even noticed? I think I might have mentioned that he shouldn't look my way and draw any attention to me. Had he actually listened to my advice for once?

"You get me the cat and no one gets hurt," Rupert muttered as we walked away from the seawall. We moved past a parking garage toward the business area. No one gave us a second glance. Either they didn't want to see or I was a great actress. But, with every step I took, my fear became greater.

Suddenly, Rupert stopped and turned. Anxiety twisted inside me as I waited to see what would happen next. He kept his gun jabbed into me.

He glowered into the distance. "You can stop following us."

I glanced at the empty sidewalk behind us and thought Rupert might be crazy. He seemed to be talking to a tree, a mailbox, and a bus stop.

"One wrong move, and I'll shoot your girlfriend," he continued. "Come out. I know you're there."

Someone stepped out from behind a tree with hands raised in the air. It was Chad. He *had* noticed I was gone.

His gaze caught mine, sending silent messages of concern before his eyes swerved back to Rupert. "Why don't you just let her go? Take me instead?"

Rupert chuckled. "That would be nice and cozy, wouldn't it? Get up here. Walk with us. Remember, I'm not afraid to use this gun. One wrong move and she dies."

Chad joined me. I didn't know whether to shake him or hug him. So I did neither, of course. Instead, we walked side by side. I could feel the tension radiating off of him. I only hoped he'd called the police before Rupert spotted him.

"You're not going to get away with this," I muttered, like any good victim might say.

"Famous last words," he smirked. We turned at an alley, passed a dumpster, and stopped by a rusty metal service door. He gave Chad a key. "Unlock it."

Chad did as he was told.

Then Rupert nudged me toward the black abyss inside. A musty smell drifted out, making it obvious the place had been abandoned. "In here."

Against my better judgment, I stepped inside. Chad was right behind me. Before the door fully closed and the light was shut out, I caught a glimpse of something in the distance. A cage. Like someone might keep a bear in while transporting it from the wild to be center ring at a traveling carnival.

"You're getting in there, and I'm taking your boyfriend to get that cat. If anything goes wrong, I'll kill you both. Understand?"

"Yeah," I muttered.

An emergency light added a sickly yet dim glow to the area. It buzzed and flickered overhead. I could barely make out Rupert's face.

He snatched the purse off my shoulder and threw it into the dark recesses of the warehouse. Out of reach. Any chances I'd had of grabbing my phone were now gone.

He looked at Chad and pointed the gun at him now. "You're going to go with me to get that cat. You moved him from your apartment," Rupert continued. "So you can take me to him now."

"Then I moved him again," I added.

Chad glanced at me. "You did?"

I nodded. "I found a nice home for Mr. Mouser."

Rupert aimed the gun at Chad's head. Then he looked at me. "Now, tell me where that cat is or he'll be my next victim."

Chad's eyes widened. He stared at me, waiting to

see what I'd do.

Did he actually think I'd choose a cat's life over his? Somewhere along the way, I'd been a terrible, terrible communicator.

My pulse quickened. "Put the gun down. I'll tell you, but only if you promise not to hurt Chad."

"Good girl." He lowered the gun. "Start talking."

"The cat is at a friend's house." *I'm so sorry, Mr. Mouser.* "But this friend may not be home. I don't know where he is. I can't get in."

"Your boyfriend better figure out a way. Otherwise you'll both have an early date with death." He shoved me. "Now, get in the cage."

I suddenly knew how this would play out. Chad would get the cat, Rupert would kill Chad, and then he'd leave me here to die like a forgotten circus animal.

I had to think fast and keep him talking. "You're really putting me in an animal cage?"

He smiled. "Ironic, isn't it?"

"I can be the one to show you the way to my friend's house." I wasn't sure what that would accomplish, but at least I could buy more time.

Rupert chuckled. "Oh no. You're too smart. You need to stay here."

"What are you saying? That I'm dumb?" Chad mumbled.

Rupert ignored him.

"I was going to let you use it for your next demonstration outside of one of those pet stores. But maybe it will serve a better purpose right now."

I stepped inside. The place smelled like rust and urine. I didn't want to think about what had happened in here. "The only reason you could possibly want that cat is if he had something on him. I'm guessing that Sage has some kind of microchip on Mr. Mouser. Maybe on his collar? That would be the safest place she could think of to keep information like that, given how Mr. Mouser is pretty much vicious."

Rupert closed the cage with a sharp *clang* and snapped a padlock in place. "Smart thinking. Now give me that address."

"492 Wilmington," I admitted. The words tasted bitter as they left my lips.

As I leaned against the bars, something jabbed me in my hip. What was in my pocket?

That's when I realized I had that awful shock collar there.

It was the only weapon of any sort I had as an option right now. But how would I get to it? How would I use it?

Thankfully, it was dark in here. It would make it easier to conceal what I was doing. I stepped out of the reach of that sickly emergency light. Then I reached into my pocket and flipped the switch on the collar, so I'd know it was on.

"I'm going to take your little boyfriend to get the cat. You better hope it's there, otherwise—" He made a little motion to indicate he'd shoot Chad.

I looked at Chad across the way. I hoped my gaze conveyed to him that I had a plan and that he should be on guard. I thought he might be able to see me, but the shadows made me uncertain. The darkness made everything look so gritty and menacing.

"Let's go." Rupert motioned to Chad.

"Wait!" I shouted. I pressed my face between the bars.

Rupert paused. "What is it?"

"I need to tell you something."

He sighed. "About what?"

"About Andre King."

"Yes, I twisted his words on my product endorsement. He's never forgiven me and threatened to sue. Thankfully, he can't find me. I'm a chameleon like that."

I leaned closer. "What about Thyme? Is she in on this?"

"I would never trust that woman with a secret. I tried to let all of that family drama work to my advantage. But never would I pull them into one of my schemes, only if I had a death wish."

"There's one more thing. Chad can't hear, though."

"What is it now?" He sounded irritated.

I lowered my voice. "Promise me you keep Chad alive and I'll tell you how you can ruin Anise, even in death."

My heart pounded in my ears. I hoped my plan worked. For everyone's sake.

He crept close to the cage. I leaned closer. He seemed to take the bait, though he looked irritated.

I flung one arm from one opening in the bars. I slapped the collar around his neck, grabbed it with my other hand, and quickly fastened it. As he yelled out, he was zapped.

Cruel, huh?

Rupert would say so.

That's how the collars worked. The more you barked, the more you got zapped.

Rupert turned toward me, his eyes wide and frightened. He had no idea what was going on. He grabbed the collar, yelling. Each time he shrieked, a shock ran through him, delaying any efforts to pull the collar off. A vicious, but effective cycle.

Chad grabbed his gun and raised it toward Rupert. Just then, the doors burst open. "FBI!"

I spotted my friend, Special Agent Chip Parker, leading the charge. How had the feds known to come? They invaded the space like hornets retaliating after their nest had been disturbed.

As some local police handcuffed Rupert, Chad handed the gun over to a uniformed officer.

Chad rushed to the cage and grabbed my hand. "Are you okay?"

I nodded. "Better now."

"I called Parker when I heard what you were up to. I thought the FBI should be close by, just in case something went wrong—or in case something went right. I had to play it safe, even if that meant you were mad at me. I couldn't live with myself if you ended up dead."

"You were trying to protect me just like I was trying to protect my cats."

He nodded. "You'd do anything for them."

"Just like you'd do anything for me. Out of love."

He squeezed my hand, and the look in his eyes said it all. All along he'd loved me. I'd been so blinded by my concern over my cats.

"I'm sorry, Chad," I whispered.

"Me, too."

Parker tossed Chad the keys to the cage, just as some local police read Rupert his rights. Chad managed to release the padlock and the door squeaked open.

I rushed into Chad's outstretched arms just as Parker walked up. The Brad Pitt look-a-like was a great law enforcement officer, but a terrible boyfriend. I'd heard all about him from Gabby. Still, I was grateful he was here.

"You okay, Sierra?" he asked.

I nodded, remaining in Chad's arms. "Fine. Thanks

to Chad. And you."

If Chad hadn't shown up, Rupert would have probably put me in the cage until I told him where the cat was. Then he would have left me there. Who would have found me in a deserted warehouse? I shuddered. I didn't want to think about what could have been.

"This guy is wanted for fraud in five states," Parker said. "We've been trying to track him down and find out his real identity."

That didn't surprise me. "You might want to question him in the murder of Ernest Wentworth," I added.

Parker raised an eyebrow. "Good to know."

"At least he won't be scamming anyone anytime soon. And maybe Sage will get some of that justice she was seeking."

"It's about time." Parker nodded our way. "Good work, you two."

"What can I say? No one's ever told me that the cat had my tongue."

Chad and Parker chuckled.

Whoever thought that could work to my advantage?

CHAPTER 20

Chad and I were questioned for a couple of hours on everything we knew about Rupert. When we were finally cleared to go, Chad and I walked hand and hand to his van. Yes, the police had let us drive down to the station.

Right now, he pulled to a stop in front of the bay. Wordlessly, we walked over the dunes and stood on the shore. The sand was soft beneath our feet, and my hope rose and then descended just like the waves in the distance.

Finally, I started. "You remember that butterfly that started all of this?"

"The Hessel's Hairstreak?"

I smiled. "That's the one. Did I ever tell you why I like butterflies so much?"

"I don't think so."

"I like them because they represent the catharsis of change. We all have the power to transform our lives. We can't change the past or what we were. But we can use our experiences to help mold us into the people we want to be today and tomorrow."

"That's really beautiful."

A soft breeze brushed my hair out of my face. "I think I've always had this deep seated fear that every man was like my dad. He never accepted me for who I really was. He wanted me to be who he wanted me to be. When you started fussing about my cats, I had so many memories of growing up and being unable to please my parents."

"I don't want you to change, Sierra." He squeezed my arm.

"I know that. I really do. I'm sorry I've been acting the way I have. My emotions got the best of me."

"I haven't exactly been a saint." He pulled me closer. "You really would choose me over your cats, when it comes down to it. You proved that."

"Of course I would. I'm sorry I let you think otherwise." I rested my hand on his chest. "Chad, I've been miserable this week without you. Like, totally miserable. I'm sorry that I wasn't more compromising. I'm my own worst enemy sometimes."

"I could have been more gracious, Sierra." He shrugged and rubbed his chin. "I don't know what got into me, either. I just felt like I'd always be second place in your life, and I couldn't stand that thought. I felt like your cats and their safety would always take first place."

"You'll always come first for me, Chad. In fact . . ." I wasn't sure what I was doing. But, somehow I ended up down on one knee. Before I could stop myself, I plunged ahead. "Chad Davis, will you marry me?"

His eyes widened. "You're proposing? To me?"

I shrugged. "I guess I am. I don't have a ring or anything but the male species don't generally wear an engagement ring."

"And the female species don't usually get down on one knee."

Uh oh. Was there rejection in that statement? I started to rise when his arms caught me and pulled me up. "I just meant that I'd rather have you up here in my arms."

"You would?" Why did I suddenly feel very insecure and young?

"Yes, Sierra Nakamura, I will marry you."

"Really?" I hadn't meant to sound so surprised. But I was surprised. This whole thing was surprising, even to me, and I'd started it.

He cupped my face with his hands. "On one condition."

"What's that?"

His eyes sparkled. "Let's get married right now."

"Are you serious?"

"Totally serious. Sierra, I can't see my future without you. I've been out of my mind this week thinking about not being with you."

"Me too!"

"In fact, I was going to propose to *you* this week. I kept getting interrupted. Then we started fighting."

I gasped. "That's what you were wanting to talk about? I had no idea."

"You got it." He reached into his pocket. "I even have this."

A ring glistened in the sunlight. It was the most beautiful thing I'd ever seen. Golden. Simple. Symbolic.

Chad slipped it onto my finger and grinned. "It's official now."

"Oh, Chad. I love it." I couldn't stop staring at it. I was engaged. Really engaged!

What would my parents think about this? They wouldn't like it. But, at the moment, I didn't care. I knew Chad was right for my life.

Chad stroked my cheek. "So, I say we ditch the whole traditional idea. We go to the Justice of the Peace, get hitched, and live happily ever after. Someone just told me today there are some great deals to Mexico this time of year."

I didn't mention that was because it was hurricane

season. Instead, I nodded. "I can wrap up my puppy mill story, turn the information over to animal control, go to Sage's funeral, and be ready by tomorrow afternoon. But what about Trauma Care?"

"Gabby is coming back tomorrow. We can call and confirm, but I know that's what she said. What do you think? Can you take some time off work?"

"Considering the founder will be locked up for a while? I think so."

He intertwined his fingers with mine. "Let's do it then."

"You really think we've got what it takes to make this work?"

"I do. You?"

I didn't have to think too hard before nodding. "I do."

Chad grinned. "That was great practice. Now let's go say our real 'I dos.'"

***

Six hours later, we stood on the beach in front of Chad's apartment. Pastor Randy stood in front of us. He'd agreed to officiate, but only if Chad and I both promised to give his church a try. We'd said yes. Maybe it was time for some changes in my life. I wasn't sure what those changes would look like yet, but I did know that I needed to be more open. I needed to be quicker to listen and slower to speak. I needed to be more about people and relationships than projects.

Sharon, one of my friends who owned a coffeehouse, and Donnie stood in as witnesses. Each held one of my cats. Sharon had Freckles, who'd been found at a local pound. I'd rushed to pick her up before the wedding. Donnie, meanwhile, held Mr. Mouser, whom he'd fallen in love with. Once I'd realized Donnie was clean, I knew I'd be able to arrange a love connection between the grieving cat daddy and the grieving Mr. Mouser. I'd dropped the cats off at his place last night and today Mr. Mouser wanted nothing to do with me already. He was all about Donnie.

It also turned out that Pastor Randy kind of liked cats. He was going to cat sit for me while I was on my honeymoon. I might even be able to talk him into becoming a cat foster daddy. He'd be great at it.

I wore my one and only dress, a yellow billowy number, with spaghetti straps. Chad wore a white button up shirt, untucked, with khakis. A lovely breeze blew in from the ocean, and, for a moment, I forgot what really made the bay smell like it did. The sunset smeared colors across the sky all around us.

This was going to be the best day and worst day of my life, all wrapped into one. The best day because I was marrying the love of my life. The worst day because I'd almost died.

"Sierra, for your vows, I heard you'd like to speak from your heart?" Randy started.

I nodded and squeezed Chad's hands. "Chad Davis, I promise to always love you more than my cats. I promise that you'll be my first priority. I promise that, though I will never cook you meat, I will always do my best to take care of you. For better or for worse. When we're getting along like cats and dogs or getting along like lovebirds."

"Most beautiful words you've ever said to me, Sierra."

The pastor grinned. "And you, Chad?"

Chad shifted, a serious look in his eyes. "And I, Chad Davis, promise that I will always allow you to be who you are, Sierra Nakamura. I will never ask you to change, but I will love you for you. When I mess up—because, since I'm human, I will mess up—I hope that you'll forgive me. I hope that our relationship will be like a Hessel's Hairstreak butterfly. That we'll continue, as a couple, to grow into a more and more beautiful creation."

My eyes filled with tears. "That really was beautiful, Chad."

He rubbed my cheek with the back of his hand. "I mean it. Every word."

"I now pronounce you husband and wife. You may kiss the bride."

Chad's lips met mine. I couldn't believe how much I loved the idea of a happily ever after, but I truly had hope for one now.

And to think . . . the creature I had to thank for putting this all into motion was an allergenic hypoallergenic cat named Mr. Mouser.

###

Don't Miss These Books in the Squeaky Clean Mystery Series:

Hazardous Duty
She always wanted to be a forensic pathologist. But when circumstances force her to drop out of school, Gabby St. Claire starts a crime-scene cleaning business. Suddenly a routine job turns up a murder weapon, and Gabby and her neighbor Riley realize that the wrong man is behind bars! Will they catch the real killer?

Suspicious Minds
Rock and roll may never die, but the King is definitely dead... again.

In this smart and suspenseful sequel to *Hazardous Duty*, crime-scene cleaner Gabby St. Claire finds herself stuck doing mold remediation to pay the bills. But her first day on the job, she uncovers a surprise in the crawlspace of a dilapidated home: Elvis, dead as a doornail and still wearing his blue suede shoes. How could she possibly keep her nose out of a case like this?

It Came Upon a Midnight Crime
Someone is intent on destroying the true meaning of Christmas—at least, destroying anything that hints of it. All around crime-scene cleaner Gabby St. Claire's hometown, anything pointing to Jesus as the "reason for the season" is being sabotaged. The crimes become more twisted as dismembered body parts are found at the vandalisms. Who would go to such great lengths to dampen the joy and hope of Christ's birthday? Someone's determined to destroy Christmas... but Gabby St. Claire is just as determined to find the Grinch

and let peace on earth and goodwill to men prevail.

Organized Grime
Gabby St. Claire knows how to clean up scum. She can get blood out of carpet, pick shattered bones from plaster, and clean up other less-than-enticing fluids from nearly any surface. St. Claire also knows how to clean up another kind of scum— the scum of the earth. Crime scene cleaner and wannabe forensic investigator Gabby St. Claire knows her best friend, Sierra, isn't guilty of killing three people in what appears to be an ecoterrorist attack. But Sierra has disappeared, her only contact a frantic phone call. Crime scene evidence Gabby discovers while cleaning tie seemingly random murders together—and point to Sierra as the guilty party. Just what has her animal-loving friend gotten herself into? If that's not disturbing enough, who's the person following Gabby? A federal agent who hopes Gabby will lead him to Sierra? Or someone with more sinister plans? To find Sierra and prove her innocence, Gabby will have to rely on all of her training and abilities, plus the help of a man she loves and the protection of a God she's only recently begun to believe in.

The Scum of All Fears
"I'll get out, and I'll get even."

Gabby St. Claire is back to crime-scene cleaning, at least temporarily. With her business partner on his honeymoon, she needs help after a weekend killing spree fills up her work docket. She quickly realizes she has bigger problems than finding temporary help.

A serial killer her fiancé, a former prosecutor, put

behind bars has escaped. His last words to Riley were: *I'll get out, and I'll get even.* Pictures of Gabby are found in the man's prison cell, and Riley fears the sadistic madman has Gabby in his sights.

Gabby tells herself there's no way the Scum River Killer will make it across the country from California to Virginia without being caught. But then messages are left for Gabby at crime scenes, and someone keeps slipping in and out of her apartment.

When Gabby's temporary assistant disappears, Gabby must figure out who's behind these crimes. The search for answers becomes darker when Gabby realizes she's dealing with a criminal who's more than evil. He's truly the scum of the earth, and he'll do anything to make Gabby and Riley's lives a living nightmare.

To Love, Honor, and Perish
How could God let this happen?

Just when crime scene cleaner Gabby St. Claire's life is on the right track, the unthinkable happens. Gabby's fiancé, Riley Thomas, is shot and remains in life-threatening condition only a week before their wedding.

Gabby is determined to figure out who pulled the trigger, even if investigating puts her own life at risk. But as she digs deeper into the facts surrounding the case, she discovers secrets better left alone. Doubts arise in her mind and the one man with answers is on death's doorstep.

An old foe from the past returns and tests everything Gabby is made of—physically, mentally, and spiritually.

Will her soul survive the challenges ahead? Or will everything she's worked for be destroyed?

You Might Also Enjoy:

Death of the Couch Potato's Wife (Book 1, Suburban Sleuth Mysteries)
You haven't seen desperate until you've met Laura Berry, a career-oriented city slicker turned suburbanite housewife. Well-trained in the big city commandment, "mind your own business," Laura is persuaded by her spunky 70-year-old neighbor Babe to check on another neighbor who hasn't been seen in days. She finds her neighbor, Candace Flynn, wife of the infamous "Couch King," dead, and at last has a reason to get up in the morning in suburbia: murder. Someone's determined to stop her from digging deeper into the death of her neighbor, but Laura is just as determined to figure out who's behind the death-by-poisoned-pork-rinds.

The Trouble with Perfect
Since the death of her fiancé two years ago, novelist Morgan Blake's life has been in a holding pattern. She has a major case of writer's block, and a book signing in the small mountain town of Perfect sounds like just the solution to help her clear her head. Her trip takes a wrong turn when, on her way there, she's involved in a hit and run—she's hit a man, and he's run from the scene. Before fleeing, he mouthed the word "help." She plans to give him that help, but first she must find him. In Perfect, she finds a town that offers everything she's ever wanted. But is something sinister going on behind the town's cheery exterior? Was she invited as a guest of honor simply to do a book signing? Or was she lured to town for another purpose—a deadly purpose?

The Good Girl
Tara Lancaster can sing Amazing Grace in three harmonies, two languages, and interpret it for the hearing impaired. She can list the Bible canon backward, forward, and alphabetized. And the only time she ever missed church was at seventeen because she had pneumonia and her mom made her stay home. But when her life shatters around her and her reputation is left in ruins, Tara decides escape is the only option. She flees halfway across the country to dog-sit, but the quiet anonymity she needs isn't waiting in her sister s house. Instead she finds a knife with a threatening message, a fame-hungry friend, a too-hunky neighbor, and evidence of...a ghost? Following all the rules has gotten her nowhere. And nothing she learned in Sunday school can tell her where to go from there.

Home Before Dark
Nothing good ever happens after dark.

Those were the words country singer Daleigh McDermott's father always repeated.

Now her father is dead, and Daleigh fears she's returned home too late to make things right. As she's about to flee back to Nashville, she finds a hidden journal belonging to her father. His words hint that his death was no accident.

Small town mechanic Ryan Shields is the only one who seems to believe that Daleigh may be on to something. Her father trusted the man, but Daleigh's instant attraction to Ryan scares her. She knows her life and career, however dwindling it might be, are back in

Nashville and that her time in the sleepy North Carolina town is only temporary.

As Daleigh and Ryan work to unravel the mystery, it becomes obvious that someone wants them dead. They must rely on each other—and on God—if they hope to make it home before the darkness swallows them whole.

Home Before Dark offers a blend of Nicholas Sparks meets Mary Higgins Clark, a mix of charming small town life in North Carolina tangled in a gripping suspense.

About the Author

Christy Barritt is an author, freelance writer and speaker who lives in Virginia.

She's married to her Prince Charming, a man who thinks she's hilarious—but only when she's not trying to be. Christy's a self-proclaimed klutz, an avid music lover who's known for spontaneously bursting into song, and a road trip aficionado. She's only won one contest in her life—and her prize was kissing a pig (okay, okay... actually she did win the Daphne du Maurier Award for Excellence in Suspense and Mystery also... and a couple of others, but she'd hate to brag). Her current claim to fame is showing off her mother, who looks just like former First Lady Barbara Bush.

When she's not working or spending time with her family, she enjoys singing, playing the guitar, and exploring small, unsuspecting towns where people have no idea how accident-prone she is.

For more information, visit her website at: www.christybarritt.com.

Other Books by Christy Barritt

Squeaky Clean Mysteries:
#1 Hazardous Duty
#2 Suspicious Minds
#2.5 It Came Upon a Midnight Crime
#3 Organized Grime
#4 Dirty Deeds
#5 The Scum of All Fears
#6 To Love, Honor, and Perish
#7 Mucky Streak (coming soon!)
#8 Foul Play (coming soon!)

Suburban Sleuth Mysteries:
#1 Death of the Couch Potato's Wife

Stand-Alone Romantic-Suspense:
Keeping Guard
The Last Target
Race Against Time
Ricochet
Key Witness
Lifeline
High-Stakes Holiday Reunion
Desperate Measures (coming soon!)

Standalone Romantic Mystery:
The Good Girl

Suspense:
The Trouble with Perfect
Home Before Dark

Printed in Great Britain
by Amazon